THE
PAGES BETWEEN US

D0289718

THE PAGES BETWEEN US

Lindsey Leavitt
Robin Mellom

HARPER
An Imprint of HarperCollinsPublishers

The Pages Between Us

Copyright © 2016 by Lindsey Leavitt, LLC, and Robin Mellom

All rights reserved. Printed in the United States of America. No part of this book may be used or reproduced in any manner whatsoever without written permission except in the case of brief quotations embodied in critical articles and reviews. For information address HarperCollins Children's Books, a division of HarperCollins Publishers, 195 Broadway, New York, NY 10007.

www.harpercollinschildrens.com

Library of Congress Control Number: 2015947490

ISBN 978-0-06-237772-2

Interior Design by Abby Dening

Doodle Artwork by Abby Dening

16 17 18 19 20   OPM   10 9 8 7 6 5 4 3 2 1

First paperback edition, 2017

To Ashley, #2, Ali, Heather, Libby, Rachel (x2), & Shannan
for helping me turn the page and start this new chapter.
—Lindsey

To BFFs everywhere.
Best friends make us happy, healthy, and stronger.
I'm grateful for mine.
—Robin

FRENCH CLASS

Nom: <u>**Piper**</u> La Date: <u>**12 septembre**</u>

MATCHING

Draw a line from the number to the correct word in French.

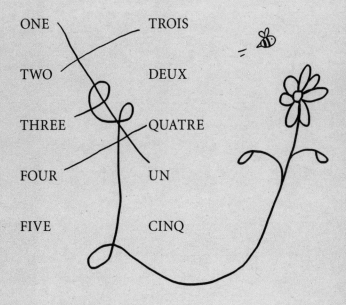

ONE   TROIS

TWO   DEUX

THREE   QUATRE

FOUR   UN

FIVE   CINQ

French Class Notes:
  French words
  Other French words
  Frenchy stuff
  Is this working?
  I'm hungry. Really wanting French fries now.

There's no need to read any further. This is just a regular French notebook.

Move along.

Seriously. Anything beyond this page is just super boring and in a totally different language. If you speak French, then this is written in some other language that you don't know.

Clipping toenails is more fun than this dumb book.

Yawn.

Really, you're just embarrassing yourself now.
Close the notebook.

Move along.

There you go.

Whew. I think it's safe now.

Turn the page ONLY if your name is Banana
Noodle or Orange Snickerdoodle...

Dearest Banana Noodle,

Of course, that's not your real name, just like my real name isn't Orange Snickerdoodle. But there's a reason why I'm calling you that. A very good reason.

Secret identities. I'm thinking we should have them in case anyone ever discovers this notebook. Do you like how I added all that French stuff to cover our bases? Now we just need trench coats and magnifying glasses. No, wait, that's spies, right? Or detectives maybe.

Anyway, Banana Noodle. You are holding this notebook because I had the best idea. The best. I think best ideas are like gifts, and recognizing them is like saying thank you to the Idea Fairy. That's a thing, right?

Last night, I escaped to Target with Mom because my dad wanted me on Twin Patrol. Talin was at piano and Luke had volleyball, and since I have no special skills, I was in charge of bathing the twins for the third night in a row. And usually I don't mind, but Flynn didn't get to the potty in time and . . . I won't share the details. So I told Dad I needed to have girl talk with Mom. The "talk" basically involved me saying, "Hey, can I buy deodorant?" and her answering, "Sure." That's it.

Thank you, sweat, for the bonding opportunity.

Because it's October and fall is already in full swing, all of the school supplies were seventy-five percent off. My mom will buy anything at Target for seventy-five percent off—school supplies, odd-sized shoes, potato chips in weird flavors. Have I ever shown you the cupboard in our house full of random stuff that she somehow puts together into those thoughtful gift baskets? I promise, someone somewhere will get a glue stick and pickle-flavored potato chips from her and be super excited about it.

But back to us. You know it was fate when I spotted the only notebook left without a stupid teen celebrity on the cover. The blue sparkles called to me and said, "*Piper . . . I mean, Orange Snickerdoodle, I belong to you. I am the most fabulous way for you to communicate with your best friend now that you're in middle school and share only ONE SINGLE CLASS. One single class after two years of sharing homeroom teachers, pencils,* everything. *Hours and hours of quality friendship time cut down to fifty-two little minutes. But! In these pages, you can describe all the details of your separate worlds—Banana, in your super-smart-kids classes, and*

Orange, in your super-regular-kids classes. I am your connec-
tion, your lifeline. Come to me, Orange Snickerdoodle. Buy me.
You hear only the sound of my voice and you must obey . . ."

Well, I grabbed the notebook, THIS notebook, before it hypnotized me completely. And then I turned on my manners. Which, you know, wasn't easy.

"Mother." Here I batted my eyes. "May I ask if you would mind purchasing me this lovely notebook?"

Mom didn't even look up. She was shoving glue sticks in our cart like they were gold nuggets in the California gold rush. "I can get you notebooks from Doodle Bugs."

"Even with your employee discount, the stationery store won't be as cheap as this."

She paused, coming up with another argument. "I just bought you notebooks for school last month."

"Right. This wouldn't be for school. This would be . . . a positivity notebook. So I can . . . be more positive?"

Mom finally stopped her "Eureka! Glue!" moment. "How do you plan to do that?"

"I'm not sure. That's why I need this notebook. So I can explore my positive side. I think I'll start with listing all the things that make my mom the coolest mom in the world. And if not the world, then in this aisle at Target."

Mom cracked a grin. "Drop it in the basket."

Which is my favorite answer.

Olivia, I mean, Banana . . . I mean . . . okay. Let's ditch the code names. Olivia—this is what we've been looking for. We suffer from the Wrath of Principal Dawn if we text in school. And how can we ever forget the Mammoth Note Scandal of Fourth Grade when Mrs. Shipley read our note *out loud* debating which underwear brand had the best elasticity? Although I'm sure everyone secretly agreed that Hanes is the way to go, it still wasn't fun being called the Undies Sisters for two whole months afterward.

But now? Our problem is solved! We can say this is a *school* notebook and pass it back and forth and no one will know! We are SO clever. The only thing keeping us away from being CIA operatives is the glitter on this cover. Although I bet CIA operatives would add glitter too, just to throw people off.

Okay, so that's all I really have. *Ta-da!* A notebook. Now we need to figure out what we're going to write.

I know the first thing you'll want to discuss is our future because we are BEST FRIENDS FOREVER. You know, going to the same college, getting jobs in the same town, buying houses on the same street, riding same-brand bikes with our same-age kids.

Let's hammer out some details on the double wedding first. Last time we talked about it, you said you wanted an empire waist dress, whatever that means. And my mom, of course, will design the invitations. We can have pansies or poppies or whatever flower you like. Those details aren't important to me.

What I'd rather discuss is the romance between our caterer and the best man. The problem is, the wedding planner was in love with him before she joined the Peace Corps. She's back now and will stop at nothing to get her man. Even if it means POISONING the caterer!

Sorry. It's possible I've watched one too many episodes of *Love and Deception*, the greatest soap opera in the history of storytelling. And by "one too many" I mean every single episode. Remind me to tell you what Randall Menard did in the last episode. Hint: it involves pure evil. And a wig.

I'm open to talking about other stuff. Although, if I can just get a vote in, let's keep the Jackson Whittaker notes down to three a day. Just to mix it up a teeny bit.

Try, Olivia—just try.

Your favorite person,

Orange Snickerdoodle

(aka Piper. Unless you are a notebook thief, in which case, GIVE IT BACK AND NEVER SPEAK OF THIS AGAIN. *Merci*.)

P.S.—Remember in fifth grade when we had to keep actual grateful journals and write five things we were grateful for in them each day? And you always wrote Jackson, Jackson, Jackson, Jackson, and "rhymes with Tackson"?

Well, whatever. I'm starting again. Today my grateful entry is:

Target sales, best ideas, deodorant, glitter, and snickerdoodles. (Why did I have to do food names? I'm so hungry now.)

Dear Brilliant-Yet-Hungry Piper,

This notebook is exactly what we need. I was hoping that formal complaint I wrote to the principal would fix all of this. But, no. Not even that quality paper from your mom's stationery store that I used changed Principal Dawn's mind about redoing our schedules. Who could refuse a request written on eco-friendly cardstock? Especially one with a Jolly Rancher attached?

I guess someone with a grape-flavoring allergy. (Whoops.)

Anyway. I still don't understand why we only have one out of seven classes together when the statistical probability is in our favor.

If there are four hundred fifty-six students in our middle school . . .

with approximately twenty-seven students per class . . .

factoring in my three accelerated classes . . .

but subtracting our French elective, then logically the average shared class would be 2.267.

Or something totally close to that.

I think whoever invented middle schools was not great at math. And they certainly were never a person like me who is scared of change and predatory birds. (Predatory birds have nothing to do with this, but I did want to mention my raptor concerns.)

You and I have always had class together.

But now? It's like a Deserted Island with No Cell Phone Reception. I was considering scraping *S.O.S.* into the dirt on the soccer field, so this notebook came at the right time.

But I do like your idea of being positive. So let's look at our plan to be BEST FRIENDS FOREVER!

What if we lived in a duplex? We could tap in code on the walls at night.

If we marry brothers, can I please have the tall one? Or the one who is a gourmet cook? Being wonderful is super necessary, too.

The double wedding! I'm so glad you remembered our bouquets of flowers that start with a *p*. (Peonies. Very classy.) I think it's interesting that you always care so much about the backstory of our wedding guests and all the staff people and not so much about the wedding itself. And, thankfully, it seems you gave up on the zombie theme.

Okay, back to the reality of middle school. There actually

is one thing that I love: French class. My favorite part, besides seeing you, is Mademoiselle Carter's glares. She has so many different kinds. The say-that-in-French glare, the don't-be-late glare, the do-not-giggle-when-you-say-*oui* glare.

She's very glary at you in particular. I'm guessing it's because she hasn't gotten over the first day when you asked her if you could go to the bathroom . . . in Spanish.

Let's discuss Monday night. Miss Jill said we're going to be assigned Trigger. He got off his leash when the new girl was working with him and he tried to run out to the parking lot and jump in a minivan. So she told me Trigger was all ours now.

Here's the note she left me last week:

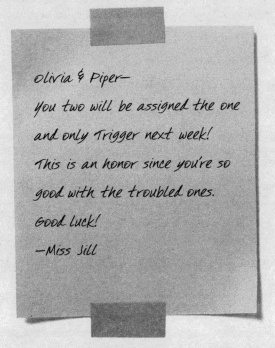

Olivia & Piper—
You two will be assigned the one
and only Trigger next week!
This is an honor since you're so
good with the troubled ones.
Good luck!
—Miss Jill

ADOPTION CARD

MY NAME IS

TRIGGER—*I'm special!!*

FACTS ABOUT TRIGGER

Breed: English bulldog mix

Color: White/gray

Sex: Male

Age: Adult

SPECIAL DETAILS: *Trigger loves to eat and lie in the sunshine. He's also a champion sleeper due to some hearing impairments. He loves to go for walks, but he has an unusual dislike for tennis shoes. Be prepared and always wear work boots! Trigger also dislikes cats, television, heavy rain, and when you say the word "come." Likes to sniff . . . sometimes excessively.*

Oh, speaking of sniffing! Warning: this next sentence has nothing to do with sniffing around—I just couldn't think of a better way to transition to this subject. Yes, you knew it was coming . . . Jackson Whittaker.

You know how Jackson and I have never been in the same class ever and I thought it was a sign from Cupid that we just weren't meant to be together? Well, guess what Cupid did for me! (I'm going to go ahead and answer that because of time and all.)

JACKSON WHITTAKER IS IN MY MATH CLASS!!!!!

I repeat:

JACKSONWHITTAKERISINMYMATHCLASS!!!!!

Sorry to get all screamy there, but I'm sort of freaking out. There I was, innocently solving a math equation, when I happened to look up and see him standing at the door. Romantic music started playing. (In my head. My head has a wonderfully talented string section. The percussion needs some work.)

Was I dreaming? Was he an apparition, like all those ghosts in *A Christmas Carol*? Or was I just lucky?

Either way, Jackson appeared and was suddenly in a seat near-ish to mine. Even though it's October and there was no reason to explain the sudden and wonderful appearance. I don't know how that happened, but thank you, Cupid! I could hardly speak, much less solve for *x*.

So here's where you come in . . . I've gotten by fine in the past with my standard flirty questions like, "Do you know what time it is?" and "Think it will rain today?"

But if I have a class with Jackson EVERY DAY, I'm going to have to come up with other questions to ask him.

Good questions.

Cute questions.

Meant-to-be-together questions.

Questions totally unlike the time I asked Robbie Morris if the rock next to his foot was igneous or sedimentary.

Because I am now certain—more than ever—that he's the perfect guy. Here's why: over the summer, Jackson grew two whole inches. You know what that means, right? We are now exactly the same height!

Eye to eye.

Heart to heart.

CUPID IS ON THE JOB!

Got screamy there again. Sorry. (I just took a couple of deep, cleansing breaths. It helped.)

It's just that I feel like if I can't conquer my fears of finally talking to him, then how will I ever learn the other life skills I need to survive middle school?

Hold on. Mr. Marsdale is looking at me. I'm going to pretend I didn't already finish the assignment ten minutes ago so he doesn't load me with "supplementary learning."

TEN LONG MINUTES LATER.

Okay, I'm back. The period is almost over, and then I have to deal with the dreaded cafeteria. Life just isn't the same without having lunch with you. We can't make our famous Tater Tots castles on Tater Tots Tuesdays. And have miniature sword fights on French Fry Fridays.

Man, I miss elementary school.

Middle school lunches are so boring (option 1 or option 2? Come ON. No adorable descriptions?). I'm still packing my own lunches this year. Mom bought the hummus chips I asked for, but she forgot the unsweetened almond milk I put on the list. When I asked Dad what he wanted me to add to the grocery list he yelled, "Coffee and coffee!" as he dashed out the door. And Mom forgot the coffee too. It's like I'm the only adult in our house.

I shouldn't complain about all this because I already vented to Blinkie last night while I paced my bedroom floor. He's such a good listener. I'm fairly certain he blinks once for yes and twice for no. Or it could just mean he wants his litter changed.

In related news: I tell my secrets to my cat.

In double-related news: I'm the biggest nerd ever. (As my BFF, neither of these facts is actually news to you. But I felt they needed to be written down in our Super-Secret Sparkly Notebook. There should be a word for notebook that starts with *s*).

I know you hate having to be on diaper patrol with the twins and stuff, but I can't help but be jealous that you have people to talk to . . . although in your house, there are a lot of people. Practically an entire soccer team—with substitutes. But the twins are so cute. Beyond cute. They're pretty much the reason why people have kids. And one of these days I will figure out which one is which. Maybe draw a dot on their chins? Color-coding always helps me.

What did you do at lunch yesterday? Ate with massive amounts of lovely people, I'm guessing. Who wouldn't want to hang out with you? I do.

Anyway, let's just hope someone—hopefully a human— asks me to sit with them at lunch today. Yesterday, I sat with Dana Huffington and her minions. And when I say "sat with" I mean "squatted in a chair sort of near them." It was not my favorite moment.

For your entertainment, here are the details of "not my favorite moment":

I spotted an open seat near Dana and took it. Yay me! While I was trying to come up with some sort of opening remark, I studied the ridges on my chips (hummus and sea salt flavored) (they're so good).

And then I overheard one of them whisper, "Who eats hummus chips?"

"Eww," her friend said.

They all giggled and then pulled out their lunch items, spreading them out on the table. With all the food set out for display, it was almost as if they'd set up shop.

And what happened next was nothing short of amazing.

In a whir of activity, they began trading food . . .

Doritos for yogurt sticks.

String cheese for raisins.

Fruit strips for teddy bear graham crackers.

It was some secret bartering system they had created, and it felt as if I needed a secret code to belong.

All I had were my hummus chips.

I pulled my lunch bag in close and ate in silence while they all happily snacked and threw their heads back in laughter as if they were having their own fancy cafeteria cocktail party.

I couldn't help but wish that someday I'd get invited.

But, hey . . . I shouldn't complain. At least I was in a seat near other humans. Jackson would think I'm a total nerd if he ever saw me eating all alone.

Let's just hope that NEVER happens.

Meanwhile, I have to find the confidence to talk to Jackson. Cupid did all this hard work—I can't let him down.

You can help me figure out a way to talk to him, right?

RIGHT?!

Whew! There's the bell. Just in time for our next handoff. I love this notebook.

Your bestie,

Olivia

P.S. Yeah, we should probably ditch the code names. They were making me hungry too.

P.P.S. I love the boots you're wearing today.

P.P.P.S. My pants are too short again. But you knew that.

Piper,

Okay, so here is my P.P.P.P.S. (You've created a monster!)

I'm sitting in next period, and I came up with something for the notebook.

It might be amazing.

Break it to me gently if it's not, but otherwise we have to do it.

You know how I put in that note from Miss Jill about Trigger? And you know how my anthropologist dad is always trying to get me to read books on ancient civilizations and I'm always telling him I'm just a sixth grader and not a college freshman like my brother?

Well, those two thoughts collided and gave me an inspiration:

What if humans somehow became extinct two hundred years from now, and all the books and computers and everything were somehow destroyed? Except this notebook miraculously survived. All the alien anthropologists would have to study was THIS notebook . . . our words . . .

to understand the preteen experience. We would need to let all the little green aliens know about double weddings, and lunch seating problems, and the way dog adoption works, and how *Gilmore Girls* is the best show in any universe. (I will be forever indebted to Netflix for putting *GG* on my list of recommended shows "Because You Watched *Parenthood*." Even though it was my mom who streamed *Parenthood*.) We would have a responsibility to future generations—of aliens!

So let's document all this like anthropologists. One day I'll show it to my dad and he'll be proud of our scientific approach and he'll for sure be proud that I spelled it correctly the first time around.

I also forgot to add my five grateful things:

1. This brilliant notebook
2. Cupid
3. Blinkie's good listening skills
4. Open seats in the cafeteria (that's more of a "hope" than a "grateful")
5. ~~Jackson, rhymes with Tackson,~~ That guy in my math class who happens to be my same exact height

(Of course I numbered my gratefuls. I was born a list-er.)

Love ya!

Olīvīa

Olivia!

As your best friend, I'm supposed to be all calm and collected and remind you that for the Jackson you saw in your math class to be a ghost, he would have to have somehow died. And if he had, there would have been a school assembly with grief counselors. Which there was not.

So . . . yay! Jackson's in your math class—I'm so excited for you! What are the chances? (It's okay. You don't have to tell me the actual chances.) I bet his schedule changed now that he got voted into student council. If he had math the same period as leadership class, it would need to switch, right?

Wait, why am I asking YOU this? I'm sure you have his schedule memorized.

So where does Jackson sit in relation to you? Is "near-ish" within the paper-passing radius? Do you like that I just wrote *paper-passing radius*? Who's the smarty-pants now?

I wish you guys shared English instead. Then you could get in the same group and study Shakespeare and volunteer to be Romeo and Juliet together. Your hands would touch, your eyes would meet, and time would slow down while all the noises faded around you. (This is what happens with my favorite lovebirds, Ashley Desdemona and McKay Davis, on *Love and Deception*. There's also a lot of face slapping, which just seems unnecessary. Yet entertaining.)

Do we study Shakespeare in sixth grade? I don't know. Ooh! Big thought: maybe Jackson is bad at math. Maybe he'll need a tutor. And everyone knows *you* are the smartest math whiz in school. And please don't bring up that A-minus in fourth grade. No one cares.

And if he does need a tutor, you're the best. I know. Because you help me with reading comprehension stuff. I've, you know, struggled with understanding what I'm reading for a long time, but then you explained everything like it was real life, better than any teacher I've ever had. And you did it without even being paid or bribed with baked goods by my mom. Unless she did. Then our whole friendship is fake. Although for her snickerdoodles, I wouldn't blame you. Great. I'm hungry again. Okay, so, I know you are the list-er, so here goes . . .

WAYS TO CATCH YOUR LOVE BY TUTORING HIM
(which, yes, was a plotline in season eight or nine of *Love and Deception*. I have no actual experience in this. Obviously.).

   1.   Wear glasses. I know, you can still be smart and

have twenty-twenty vision. But even if they are fake glasses, they give you something to twirl, readjust, push up your nose . . . basically, glasses give you something to DO.

2. And if not glasses, then a scarf. Ashley Desdemona wears a scarf in almost all her scenes and she is the fiercest, boldest, prettiest character ever. I'll crochet you one and you can fidget with an accessory instead of counting hummus chip ridges. ☺

3. Know what you are talking about, but don't be a know-it-all.

4. Don't slump.

4.5. And don't say I sound like your mom. Guys love tall girls. Look at Taylor Clarke—she got asked out three times in one day and she's almost taller than her locker. Stand up straight, you beautiful giant!

5. I don't have a number 5, but four tips didn't seem long enough.

END SCENE

No worries about being un-positive sometimes. Positivity is a hard emotion to keep up. Especially at lunchtime, which is not my favorite time of day either.

Allow me to illustrate.

And by illustrate, I mean just tell you. Since we both know I can't draw pictures. (Bubble letters are something else.)

Bubble, in bubble letters. That's deep, right?

So our teacher let us out one minute before the bell as a reward for good behavior or something. And I didn't have to go to my locker to get my lunch. And my fourth period is across from the cafeteria. Add that all up, and what do you get?

Piper in the lunchroom! First person! Freedom!

I slid into a seat at a round table smack dab in the middle of the cafeteria. I figured, if someone sat by me, fine. If someone didn't, finer. Food is serious business for me. I just wanted to eat and not have to deal with what I was about to have to deal with. Which was—

Bethany. Livingston.

"Hey, Piper! How's class?!"

I know I said it was fine if someone sat by me . . . but it was *Bethany Livingston*. Queen blogger of all the comings and goings of Kennedy Middle School. You've got to be super peppy and involved to keep that up. And she's the president of my church youth group. I sorta feel like she's been assigned by our bishop to be nice to me, just because I sit alone in Sunday school.

Liv, why does *alone* have to be so bad? Like in all these shows and movies, there is the LONER, and everyone makes fun of them when maybe they should say, "Gee, that person is comfortable enough that they can just do their own thing and not worry about everyone else."

I do great alone. And it's not like I'm alone all the time. I have you and my family and my favorite soap opera (or, as my great-aunt calls them, my "stories"). I don't know why lunchtime has to be spent talking (not important) as well as chewing (very important).

But I did my best to make chitchat with Bethany. If I didn't, I worried she would try even *harder.* I chirped: "Class was great! I didn't understand today's assignment. And I've been hungry for a snickerdoodle for three days. How about you?"

Aren't I getting so good at sarcasm, Olivia?

"Super! My classes are sooo easy this year. Too easy. I think my mom is going to ask the teacher for enrichment work or something. Oh, hey, there's Scarlett!" (She said *enrichment*, I'm not even kidding.)

Scarlett joined us. Then Eve. And Tessa.

Bethany Livingston is one thing. But Eve was BESTIES with . . . you know . . . Savannah Swanson. And I am NOT bringing up the Savannah Swanson Incident of third grade. But. I still can't be around those girls for very long. Even if it's three years later. Even if they are in my church class. And even if they act nice to me. I will never forget how they treated you. Not ever. I am by your side, Olivia. As a real friend should be. Isn't it better to have one true best friend than a bunch of girls who you don't totally trust?

I mean, I'm still a good person. I didn't throw Tater Tots at them. But I thought about it. I sure thought about it.

So this is what they all said to me. I don't remember who said what. They kind of melt into one another, like the extras who walk in and out of the background of *Love and Deception*.

"That turkey sandwich looks so yummy!"

No it didn't. It was really a tomato sandwich with a sliver of lunchmeat because my mom ran out this morning.

"Those are cute boots!"

I'm not even sure who said it but I don't think they meant it. But when *you* say it, I know you mean it, and thank you by the way. I bought them at Justice with my babysitting money.

"Did you buy your fabric for the blanket drive yet?"

Oh, yeah. The blanket drive. It's for church service day.

I'm attaching the flyer in case you want to go. It's still a month and a half away, but I thought I should include it in case aliens two hundred years later care about flyers (great idea on being anthropiligists. Even if I can't spell anthropiligist). Our class is in charge of fleece blankets for NICU babies. All the fabric store had left was camo. I hope some poor mom doesn't wrap her baby and lose him in all that camouflage.

"Hey, Piper, we'll see you at church!"

Eve. That girl should go to church a lot because she is probably swimming in guilt over the Savannah Swanson Incident. Not to bring it up again. Did I mention I will eternally and forever have your back?

Isn't it strange that the reason I was sitting in the same space with those girls is because our parents all believe in the same things? Sharing beliefs might be a big friend-maker in the adult world, but at that lunch table, it only meant that we ran out of things to say. So they turned to one another and started to plan their next slumber party.

Which I don't even want to go to, thanks for asking.

"Oh, I saw your dad's Mr. Brake commercial last night." Eve turned toward me again. Yikes. "He's kind of famous, isn't he? Does he ever need models for his commercials? I model sometimes."

I did not have the heart to tell Eve that Dad, aka Mr.

Brake, is not her gateway to fame. He has one dorky car commercial that airs at four in the afternoon on, like, the second Tuesday of the month in a small California town. You know how much I hated all the attention when it came out, and just when I think it's over, he has an idea for another one. Who buys brakes from a guy dressed like a genie, rubbing a lamp?

I picked up the pace on my eating. Thought maybe I could run to the library for some computer time. I haven't checked the *Love and Deception* chat boards in days.

"Did you see I had EIGHTEEN comments on my last blog entry?" Bethany asked me.

I wolfed down the rest of my sandwich in two monstrous bites. I didn't even eat my Fig Newtons, that's how desperate I was to get out of there. "That's great. Uh . . . happy blogging. Bye."

"Thanks!" She smiled her automatic smile. "Peace out, Piper!"

She speaks in exclamation points. And all those exclamation points made my head hurt. Maybe people use them because of my name. Like it's naturally perky or something. Maybe when I go to college I'll rename myself something much more serious, like Eleanor.

Instead of the library, I went to the nurse's office to see if

I could lie down and get rid of my bam-bam-bamming head-ache. And even though that dark, little room smells like turkey gravy mixed with VapoRub, it was still better than sitting at that lunch table with all those exclamation points!!

Besides, Olivia. We have a pact. You know I would never, ever deal with girls like that. I like people who are nice. Like nice for real, not really nice because they are supposed to be. Yes. There is a difference.

Tell your wise cat, Blinkie, to blink once if he agrees with me: Middle School Lunch stinks.

BLINK.

See? Blinkie knows his stuff.

Peace out,

Piper!

Grateful: These boots, the cute rainbow yarn I bought at a yard sale, sounding super smart by using math words like *radius*, Mom's baking, and my dad giving me a hug today for no reason.

SOUPER SATURDAY!

SATURDAY, NOVEMBER 29
CLASSES AVAILABLE FROM 10–3

Come for a day filled with service,
sweets, and serenity!

PICK TWO OF THE FOLLOWING:

Blanket Tie for NICU babies
(hosted by youth group!)

Hygiene kits for homeless center

Care packages for the troops

Freezer dinners for Meals on Wheels

Delicious soups provided by the
activity committee.

 Bring a plate of your favorite cookies
for our annual cookie swap!

It's going to be a SOUPER day!

Piper,

Souper (Super) Saturday actually looks like it could be fun. We'll be together—it'll be fine. I may even strike up a conversation with someone I don't know! (I can't believe that sentence just came out of my pencil. We all know "striking up conversations" isn't really my thing.)

But whatever, let's go. I'll make those organic cranberry cookies you love—and I'll cram in a bunch of chocolate chips "to make them go down easier" just like you like 'em!

I'm sorry you had to spend the rest of lunch in the nurse's office enduring that turkey gravy/VapoRub smell. I know the smell well. It stinks that you had to sit next to those girls at lunch. And thanks, by the way, for always having my back.

Honestly, I think the whole Savannah Swanson Incident gave me a disease . . . Social Sickness. Which consists of me COMPLETELY REPELLING PEOPLE.

Seriously. Whenever I even TRY to start up a conversation

with a fellow middle-schooler it seems to turn into a disaster every single time. It may be due to the fact that I use phrases like "fellow middle-schooler." (Help. Me.)

So, for example, this morning when I was at my locker, Tara Long said (to no one in particular), "Oh, darn! I broke my pencil."

As luck would have it, I happened to have a finely sharpened extra pencil on me. (Three; I had three finely sharpened extra pencils. Stop laughing.)

And it would have been the perfect moment for me to say, "You can have mine, Tara." And we could have carried on from there as we walked side by side down the hall.

But what came out of my mouth?

Just a stutter of the word "you." Which sounds like this: "yuh-yuh-yuh." Don't try it, you'll hurt your tongue.

Tara turned to me looking horrified and said, "Are you choking on something?"

I waved her off as politely as possible. She whirled around and took off.

Impressive, right? She probably thinks I'm possessed by a demon. A stuttering demon.

Honestly, the only other bright spot besides French is math class with Jackson. Oh, look at that! I mentioned him already.

Here are all the necessary details:

I don't think the act of me "saying" "things" to "his face" will ever happen. That means our future wedding will be quite awkward.

So I need to lay some groundwork. I'm going to focus all my energy into getting a note to him. Jackson is almost within note-passing range.

Which means getting it to him might require the help of a middleman.

Or middlewoman.

To be specific, Jackson is one seat up and two seats over. Like, if this was a chess game and I was a knight, he'd totally be MINE.

Dad and I don't play chess as much since he went back to teaching at the university. While he was taking that year off to "do research on economic growth in Midwestern cities during the 1850s" (a phrase he constantly muttered), we played a game of chess every day. On good days, we played two.

Of course, he'd stop mid-game if Jason happened to call from school. Chatting about Jason's coursework seemed to be Dad's true passion in life. I guess I sort of assumed that he would start chatting with me as soon as Jason moved out. All I got was one to two chess games a day.

Maybe I should have been grateful for that.

Now that Dad's back to work full-time? I can hardly get the word "chess" out of my mouth before he's running out the door, gripping his mug of coffee and barely saying good-bye.

This explains why I recently Googled the phrase "Can you teach chess to a cat?"

In related news: YouTube videos of cats playing chess is A THING. And also how I lost forty-five minutes of my life.

But I did find out that you, of course, were right, and Jackson being in my math class wasn't a ghostly vision. Yes, they had to rearrange his schedule because of student council. But the best part of that news? He was voted in as class secretary. Secretary!

Secretary is such a vital part of any organization. I'd really like to read his notes sometime. I could give him some tips on when to use bullet points instead of outline form.

Anyway, since every chess player thinks two moves ahead, I was brainstorming conversation starters in case I found myself in a position to chat with Jackson.

I wrote these down on the bottom of my math worksheet.

$$\frac{3}{4} \times \frac{1}{2} = \qquad \frac{1}{5} \times \frac{2}{5} = \qquad \frac{3}{8} \times \frac{1}{3} =$$

$$\frac{2}{7} \times \frac{1}{6} = \qquad 2\frac{2}{3} \times \frac{4}{5} = \qquad 1\frac{1}{2} \times \frac{3}{4} =$$

Conversation starters!

[On the bus]
"Hi, want to sit here? I'll move over so the seat will be warm for you!"

[In the cafeteria]
"Are you going to eat your coleslaw raisins?"

[In math]
"These equations are hard. I can come over and help you!"

[In math] "Long division takes so LONG, amirite?! I can come over and help you!"

[In math]
"Can I come over? Anytime? And help you?"

Oh, sheesh, Piper! THESE ARE AWFUL.

Your idea to get a scarf and some fierce fake glasses is way better. Like a mini-makeover, tutoring style. I am sort of jealous that you wear glasses for REAL. You're halfway to becoming your favorite soap star, Ashley Desdemona.

I should probably take you shopping with me next time because my shopping experience with Mom this past weekend only resulted in the purchase of three skirts and a book, all of which I really didn't want.

Let me explain:

As soon as we got in the car, Mom rattled off all the things we were going to do for "girls' day."

"First a stop at the Tea Room for a little something to eat, honey." Her adorable Southern accent slipped out. Considering how often she tells people here in California that she's originally from Atlanta (Atlaaaaanta)—as if it's an exotic land—I'm pretty sure she likes her Southern accent to slip out. I like it too, actually.

"Already had a juice smoothie. Really, all I need are some practical pants. So can we just—"

She crinkled her nose and patted my hand. "It's girls' day, Olivia. We're having lunch, going department-store shopping, then getting our nails done and eyebrows waxed."

Waxed?! Does she think I am her forty-year-old coworker? I'm a KID.

But she looked excited so I painfully eked out a smile. I didn't know how to tell her that all I wanted to do was eat orange sorbet at Rite-Aid and go buy some sturdy slacks at the outlet mall. Mom doesn't seem to understand that I grow out of pants approximately twenty minutes after I buy them.

And then came the avalanche of questions. *How are you? Are you liking your new school now that you've been there a while? Have you found any nice people to eat lunch with? Do you need more school supplies? Skirts? Are you happy?*

You know Mom. She practically has a PhD in prying. OK, fine, maybe not prying. More like EXTREME INTEREST.

I just wish she'd ask me these things when we weren't in public. And when I wanted to share my feelings. And when there was dimmer lighting. Seriously, who opens up near fluorescent lights?

At that moment though, I really did want to tell Mom everything . . . that middle school isn't what I thought it would be. That fifty-two minutes a day is well, well below my Recommended Daily Allowance of Piper Time and I'd have scurvy if you were Vitamin C.

But instead, I clammed up. There was so much to say that I couldn't say anything at all. I shrugged my shoulders and said softly, "Fine. It's fine." Then I put an extra pat of butter on my bread.

I think Mom could sense something was wrong. My "fine" was not fine enough.

She slung her purse over her shoulder and stood up. "I know what to do."

She paid the check and led me down the sidewalk to the Happy Hearts bookstore.

She scanned up and down the aisles as if she were on an important mission. And it looked like she knew this store well.

"CarolineGrace!" The store clerk knew her name. (Her double name, because every Southern girl in Mom's family has two names jammed together. If you call me OliviaRose, I will write you out of my will, Piper.)

Mom told the clerk she needed something for "her daughter's emotional growth." Which was, of course, humiliating. They went on a hunt up and down the aisles until they spotted their treasure.

"Aha! Here it is. Some help for you." Mom placed a book in my hand. I looked at the title and shuddered. It was called *A Girl's Guide to Happiness through Southern Charm!!* And there was a double exclamation mark, as if it were written by a Dallas Cowboy cheerleader.

I . . . well, you know me Piper. I faked it. Put on a sweet smile, thanked her, and later threw it under my bed, as far back as it could go.

The book kind of haunts me at night. Am I really the kind of girl who needs advice from a self-help book? One that uses "y'all" too much?

Anyway, my mom did get excited about shopping, and I'm now the proud owner of three new A-line skirts. They're pretty cute, actually.

Okay, gotta go. I need to work on my plan for lunch today. I'm thinking about asking the counselor if she needs help filing papers. Or maybe I could help her put up inspirational posters on the wall. Like the one that says *COURAGE!* and there's a photo of a girl in an A-line skirt chatting up a group of lovely people.

And in case you didn't notice, yesterday I wore red because I was feeling spunky. Today it's yellow—the color I wear when I overthink things.

Forever at your side,

Olivia

Grateful for:

1. Famous cats who play chess
2. Pats of butter
3. The perfect side view I get of Jackson's head every day starting at 10:47
4. Your problem-solving skills (you will find a way to keep me from spending every lunch period in the counselor's office—I know you will)
5. A mom who tries

Olivia,

Your mom took you to a place called the Tea Room? I've never even had tea. It looks so gross. You stick a bunch of crushed-up leaves in a little packet and call that a drink? Mmmm, yummy, let's try dirt soup next—maybe they'll serve that at Souper Saturday.

And the book! We won't even talk about the book. But you are going to show me that book next time I sleep over, and we are going to act out scenes from the made-up conversations.

THE JOYS OF BUYING LACY UNDERGARMENTS, Y'ALL!

This is going to be the best skit ever, just wait.

That's assuming your dad has gotten over his anti-sleepovers thing. He can't still be worried about how "being off a sleep schedule isn't good for your growth" when you're now the tallest girl in our grade. (Your parents are so ~~overprotective~~ concerned.)

I just wish we lived closer to each other. I'd try biking to your house again, but the last time I tried that I only made it halfway before I had to call my dad from a random 7-Eleven. Another roadblock in our quest for Togetherness.

Speaking of Togetherness, let's talk about Jackson (oh my gosh, that sounded JUST LIKE YOU). Did you notice that I asked you about passing notes and you wrote back like you would actually do it? So do it! Go big, Olivia!

(I even wrote the first note for you, since I was coloring with my brothers and bored out of my mind. You have my permission to use this whole, or bits and pieces.)

(I don't care if you ball up the note and throw it at the boy. It would still be progress. Oh, I would be so PROUD.)

PROUD
THAT'S ME

So another school day over, and it was Mom's busy driving day. Since *someone* has soccer and *someone else* plays a musical instrument, someone (*me*) had to watch the twins. This is me stating a fact, not complaining. Regular middle children complain about these things, and we both know that even though I am in regular-kid classes, I am far from REGULAR. (Although if I did have "something to be taken to," I'd get more car time with Mom and Dad. They listen to a lot of ABBA. I love ABBA.)

So, I was told to watch the kids, and watching is exactly what I did—watched them watch their second episode of *The Pittlehorners*. That's the actual name of the show. Kid-TV-show writers must be getting desperate.

It's kind of funny, Olivia, how you are the only kid in your house and you feel alone. Because sometimes I feel the same way. Like there are all these activities happening around me. Things to do, people to see, diapers to change. And I'm just kind of . . . there. Watching it happen. Not really A PART of anything. Except dealing with the diapers, and who wants to be a part of that?

I wonder if anyone else in my family ever notices that. Doubtful. Noticing me isn't something that's written on my mom's big whiteboard of family events.

Anyway, my brothers were being pretty good. They were

halfway into their show when Flynn looked up at me with his little angel eyes and asked, "Can we get some lemonade?"

I looked in the cupboard for the barrel-size container with pink dancing lemons, but we were out. "Water's healthier. I'll get you water."

"Not from OUR house." Spencer rolled his eyes at Flynn, as if to say, *Can you believe her?* They have this secret twin eye-rolling language. Also, they are three. (Almost four. They would want me to mention that.) "Danny has a store."

Ugh, Danny Moss. Yep, *that* Danny—the one who lives seven doors down. I know you think he's cute, Livvy, but he IS NOT. He is in seventh grade and still sets up that stupid lemonade stand all the time, and our neighborhood still buys because they know if they don't, Danny will come door-to-door with his braces-free smile looking for buyers. Not that I'm keeping tabs on him.

He bought a *new skateboard* with his lemonade money, and now he annoyingly wheels around on it like he owns the street. (Again, not keeping tabs. Danny? Danny who?)

And he wouldn't let me sell brownies at his stand that one time I asked. It was to raise money for camp, not to buy my own selfish *toy*. Jerk.

The twins had already decided they were getting lemonade, so I was helpless. And I had to use the money that I got from babysitting them to buy it, which seems totally wrong, right?

"Hey, Pepper." Danny grinned at me when we walked up, like he's so cool. Cool is working at a record shop, or even Target, not a neighborhood lemonade stand that serves three-year-olds.

"Two cups, Danny." I raised my chin. I think I look in control when I do that.

"Please," Spencer added solemnly.

"Your name is *Pepper*?" Danny's friend sitting next to him sneered. There are always three or four dorks with him. I don't even know where they come from, because they don't live nearby and don't ride our bus. Danny's friends are the only thing worse than Danny. It's like he picked them to make himself look good. Which is HARD TO DO.

"Her name is Piper," Flynn said while he was drinking, lemonade dribbling down his face. Also, he pronounces my name "Pipe-Or."

This made Danny and his friends snort. Flynn looked hurt, like they were laughing at him, which they might have been, I don't know. Either way, they were being jerks.

I put my arm around Flynn. "Yeah, it's too bad I don't have a cool name that rhymes with stuff like *fanny* and *granny*."

That smile slid right off Danny's face. "Go away."

I pulled my brothers away from the table and dropped a penny in his tip jar. One cent. Which wasn't the nicest thing to do, but seriously. A TIP JAR?

"You need to work on your customer service," I said.

Danny must have agreed with me because he leaned over the table and gave the twins high fives. "Thanks for coming, little dudes. You should come over and play with my sister, Andrea, sometime."

Flynn wrinkled his nose. "Andrea is nine. We are free. Almost four."

"And Andrea is *Piper's* friend," Spencer said, like he was being helpful.

That sent the guys into a fit of hysterics. Technically, I babysit Andrea because Danny is always out selling sugared beverages when his mom needs to run an errand. She probably pays me more than Danny makes at his stand, but I'm not cluing him in on that.

And yes, I happen to get along with Andrea. We are only three years different, four years in school. My mom's best friend is ten years older than her!

So she wants to play Barbies all the time. But it's fun to create scenes from *Love and Deception*, which involves love potions, scandals, and at least one doll in a coma. We should play it sometime, Liv. I'll let you be Ashley Desdemona and Randall Menard as long as I can direct.

"Hey, Andrea is nice!" I said.

"Dork," one of the boys said.

And here we are again, because Danny is the closest kid my age in the neighborhood, while my brother Luke has four friends nearby he goes to high school with and Talin is best friends with a girl around the corner. It's like the numbers are never going to work out my way.

Not that I want new friends. I just want to clone you. That's not creepy, right?

"I would rather be a dork than be mean," I said. Not my best comeback, but it was all I could come up with right then. And then I stormed away with my brothers, Danny and his biking/skateboarding loser friends laughing as I went.

It's raining tonight. I wish it had rained on Danny's stupid stand. After I was done babysitting the twins, I played Barbies with Andrea and didn't even charge her mom.

Anyway, the note you should sign with YOUR name and pass to Jackson is attached.

Love ya like a sis (a sis who is my age and likes my company),

"Pepper"

Grateful for:

Pennies, Barbie dramas, when you get a splinter out (I had a nasty one today), my mom reimbursing my baby-sitting money, using the words "ambiance" and "reimburse" in the same letter

Hey, Jackson,

Since you are new in our math class, I thought I would send you a friendly letter with pointers on how to survive period 3. Just helping out another classmate.

1. Don't even think about getting your cell phone out. Larry Higgins had his taken away two weeks ago and still hasn't gotten it back.

2. ADD SOMETHING SMART HERE, LIV. I don't even know what you study in math. Half the kids in my class can't even multiply fractions. (Yes. I'm in that half. It's not worth it to me to deal with any number less than one.)

3. The pencil sharpener in this room is like a ferochius shark. It gobbles up pencils. If you need anything sharpened, come see me. (BTW, did I spell ferochius right?)

4. Yes, Mr. Dreadmore does smell like breakfast sausage. But sometimes he smells like syrup too, so those even out.

I don't know if you have any pets, but I work at an animal shelter once a week and we get all sorts of cool creatures coming in there. You should stop by the shelter for a visit.

Maybe you'd like to sit together at lunch sometime. You might like it. I suspect we are soulmates.

Well, write back if you get a chance. And put that cell phone away, you crazy kid!

I'm obsessed with you,
Olivia

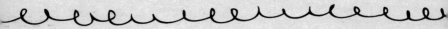

Piper,

You. Helping me write a note to Jackson. I love it! This takes off so much pressure. You wrote a lot of good stuff. Except for the parts that involve SERIOUS HONESTY. Maybe it should be less obvious? I could ease into the whole "we are soulmates" thing. But then again, what do I know about getting guys to like me? It's possible that whacking him over the head with my feelings is the way to go.

Here are my notes on your note.

TRN OVR →

great start

Hey, Jackson,

Or should this opener be more flirty? We could use words like "cute," and "lol," and "wowzers!"

Since you are new in our math class, I thought I would send you a friendly letter with pointers on how to survive period 3. Just helping out another classmate.

Also, Larry Higgins will only wear shirts that are the color green. Not that it has anything to do with the topic at hand, but it's something I've noticed.

1. Don't even think about getting your cell phone out. Larry Higgins had his taken away two weeks ago and still hasn't gotten it back.

Smart? Okay, got it: I know all about equations if you need help. My favorite ones are linear equations that are basic polynomials with a degree of one. And now I sound like A GIANT NERD. (Help.)

2. ADD SOMETHING SMART HERE, LIV. I don't even know what you study in math. Half the kids in my class can't even multiply fractions. (Yes. I'm in that half. It's not worth it to me to deal with any number less than one.)

3. The pencil sharpener in this room is like a ferochius shark. It gobbles up pencils. If you need anything sharpened, come see me.
   (BTW, did I spell ferochius right?)

No, you didn't spell it right, but your effort is adorable.

And once he smelled like black olives.
Not sure if that's important, but wanted to point it out.

4. Yes, Mr. Dreadmore does smell like breakfast sausage. But sometimes he smells like syrup too, so those even out.

Should I talk about creatures here? Boys like things that are gross and predator-ish, right?

I don't know if you have any pets, but I work at an animal shelter once a week and we get all sorts of cool creatures coming in there. You should stop by the shelter for a visit.

Piper! What if he actually DID come by sometime?

I'm hyperventilating. Jackson Whittaker . . . VISITING ME. Deep, cleansing breath, deep, cleansing breath

Maybe you'd like to sit at lunch together sometime. You might like it. I suspect we are soulmates.

Instead of saying "soulmates" maybe I should just draw some hearts? I don't want him getting a restraining order. Oh! I could draw an anatomically correct heart, like the ones they put in science books. That way, he won't know if I'm hinting at love or just really good at organ illustrations. He'd think . . . he'd wonder . . . HE'D FALL FOR ME. That, or get nauseous.

Well, write back if you get a chance. And put that cell phone away, you crazy kid!

*cough, restraining order, *cough →

~~I'm obsessed with you,~~
Olivia
⤺ perfect ending

Except after I send a note, I'll have to get the guts to talk to him in person. I don't think I have those kinds of guts, Piper. If I have any guts at all.

I can't even figure out how to put words on paper that are anywhere close to charming. That's YOUR department.

I don't mean to get all Damsel in Distress Tied to a Train Track, but I'm kind of freaking out. What if I can't figure out a way to let Jackson know I like him? The spring dance is only 154 days away!

And this is exactly the stuff I was telling Ms. Benson today while I was hanging posters in her office at lunchtime. I pressed a thumbtack into her EVERYTHING IS AWESOME! poster. There's a picture of a happy snail looking down a long runway. It's not the most hopeful photo, but I didn't tell her that because she seemed super excited about it.

"So I need to find a way to, umm . . . talk to people." I didn't tell her "people" meant "Jackson."

"We can talk about ways to make new friends, Olivia. They're called icebreaker strategies. I have a handout." Ms. Benson sipped her tea. "And lift that a little higher on the left, aaaand . . . perfect!"

"I don't think I need friends. Or a handout. I just need . . ." What did I need? "Confidence," I coughed. For some reason, saying that word brings on bronchitis.

She laughed as if she understood why that word was so hard to say. She dug through a pile of papers on her desk. Finally she found what she was looking for. "Aha! THIS is what you need. The school newsletter."

I'm not sure why, but the fact that it was a "newsletter" rather than a "handout" made me curious. That doesn't make much sense, I know. I jumped down from the stepladder anyway and took it from her.

Piper. THIS was her answer. After-school clubs. Look at this thing. ⟶

Kennedy Middle School Newsletter

Vote for Your Favorite KMS Lunch Menu

We want to hear from you! Log on to the KMS website and vote for your favorite menu options. Your votes will help us create a new menu for the coming year. Here's a sneak peak at several of your choices.

Have You Joined a Club?

At Kennedy Middle School, we believe FUN and LIFELONG FRIENDSHIPS are essential! Our staff offers VIBRANT after-school programs where students can find their PASSION. We have SO MANY clubs to choose from:

ART	**KEY**
BADMINTON	**LARPING**
CHESS	**PUZZLES**
DRAMA	**ROBOTICS**
EXTREME LEGOS	**SEA CLUB**
FORENSICS	**SIGN LANGUAGE**
FRENCH	**SPELLING BEE**
FUTURE LEADERS OF AMERICA	**STUDENT GOVERNMENT**
JAPANESE ANIMATION	**TUMBLING**
	YO-YOS

So come find your interest and there you'll find friends for a LIFETIME. Middle school ROCKS!

I'm sure you're thinking the same things I was thinking:

What's up with the excessive capitalization?

LARPing?

WHO JOINS A YO-YO CLUB???!!

Maybe, just maybe, if they had a club for ANIMAL RESCUE AND TRAINING, then I could see us fitting in. But instead, they have Forensics. Do you know what forensics is? It's studying evidence in order to solve a crime. And for a middle school club, that is very creepy.

That's exactly what I told Ms. Benson.

She waved me off. "No, silly. It's not a creepy club. It's about being a sleuth. Nancy Drew and all that. Girl power!"

She was super peppy about it. But it still didn't persuade me. So we agreed that I would come back tomorrow during lunch to alphabetize her bookshelf. I'd rather do that than have Jackson see me eating lunch alone.

Oh, no. I just had a terrible thought. What if Ms. Benson runs out of projects for me to do? Then where will I be, Piper? Every time I get near the cafeteria doors, I get one of those Immediate Stomachaches. The kind I normally get when I sneak ice cream.

We have to find a way to make sixth grade better. My digestive system can't take this!

After-school clubs . . . is that really the answer?

Ugh! We might be doomed, Piper—and that's me looking on the bright side. Imagine how down I'd be if I didn't have Jackson in my math class. Oh, look at me mentioning him twice.

Sigh.

Our only hope is to make that note to him ROCK HIS WORLD, as a certain author who wishes she was a DALLAS COWBOY CHEERLEADER would say. (I admit I PEEKED at the BOOK when I couldn't sleep last night.)(That brochure makes me want to over-capitalize now.) (Try it—it's sOrt of FuN.)

And I'm wearing purple today. Yep—feeling anxious. I'm going to go pet Blinkie and see if it helps.

Peace, love, bunnies, and UnIcoRns,

Olivia

Grateful for:

1. Ms. Benson needing projects done at lunchtime
2. When I DON'T have a stomachache
3. Unnecessary capitalizaTION
4. You helping me write that note to Jackson
5. The fact that it won't be long until we can hang out at the animal shelter

★ BETHANY'S BUSINESS ❤

HOME   NEWS   EVENTS   ABOUT   CONTACT

Hey, readers/subscribers/friends/randoms ☺
Thanks for stopping by Bethany's Business! I've
been such a bad blogger lately, I'm so sorry. But
you know I would never miss Buzz Thursday!
Here you'll find all the buzz happening at Kennedy
Middle School.

I mean, the buzz that *matters*. To me.

WHAT IS HOT

KNEE SOCKS
Totally in again, usually worn with Converse. Girls
AND boys. The wackier the better.

PACKING EXOTIC LUNCHES
Regular old PB&J is so last year. Try vegetables
fresh from the farmers' market, or Thai or
Mongolian leftovers in (recyclable) Tupperware.

Be adventurous! Seaweed chips, raw almonds, or French *macarons*.

CLUBS

School clubs officially started up last week and there are even more to choose from this year. If you haven't checked them out, you might want to think about:

1. EXTREME LEGO CLUB: Pick a partner and get LEGOing! If you join before December, you can go on the trip to LEGOLAND in San Diego!

2. SEA CLUB: This one is new this year and I helped start it! Every week, we explore different sea creatures and the ecosystem of the central California coast. Regular beach trips to Avila, Pismo, and even Santa Barbara. Also: pit stops for ice cream at Cold Stone Creamery!

3. FUTURE LEADERS OF AMERICA: I think that title says it all. I'll be joining that one for sure. No surprise there.

SHOUT OUTS

★ I sat by Piper Jorgensen the other day at lunch. She's such a sweet girl! Kind of quiet, but maybe I intimidate her. I do that a lot—I think it's because I'm so friendly.

Anyway, she had on the most adorable aqua scarf and when I asked her where she got it, she pushed up her (also adorable) blue-rimmed glasses (that she only seems to wear half the time) and said . . . *I knit it myself.*

Isn't that SO VINTAGE? I love the idea of making my own clothes, but ugh . . . I'm just so busy with volunteering and school and sports and blogging that I don't think I'd have time. But kudos to Piper! We should totally start a scarf-knitting business.

★ Is it just me, or did Jordan Goldberg kind of grow up over the summer? Jordan and I used to have playdates at the tide pools with our moms, and now he looks like he's fifteen! And I like

his shaggy hair. Jordan, if you're reading, stop
growing, but not your hair. ☺
(Totally kidding.)

★ Dana Huffington won an art contest award!
  I wish I could draw, but I have other talents.
  Anyway, that is SUPER cool, Dana. Get 'em, girl.

CELEBRITY GOSSIP

Just one but it is huge.

I hear they might film a MOVIE here with RENEE
WILDER and they are looking for EXTRAS. I have
been all over the internet trying to find info. Will let
you know what I can.

K, that's all I have for now. Hook me up with some
comments, though. I love all my readers to pieces.
LOVE, LOVE, & LOVE,
Bethany

6 COMMENTS

Danahuffhuff: Aww, thanks, girl! Come over and

draw with me anytime. Go Kennedy Middle School Harbor Seals! Woot!

Becca555: Omg! I'm TOTALLY going to join Sea Club if we get to go to Cold Stone. Their Oreo Overload makes me ☺☺☺☺.

DjTyler: @Becca555, Oreos are my favorite. I'm joining that club for sure.

Jacksondude: I'm in the LEGO Club and it's the best. I'm making my own space station with a parking garage, too.

JamieheartsScience: Knee socks are back IN?! I just threw all mine out and bought a bunch of skinny jeans. Dang it!

Bethanyblogs: Jamie, keep those skinny jeans. I predict that trend will last for a solid three more months. Thanks for reading, Bethanites! More to come!!!

Olivia,

We don't need to join a club. When have we ever needed a club? You just need to muster up the courage to talk to Jackson. Who cares about other people? Clubs sound like something Bethany Livingston and her crew would do. (According to her latest blog post I attached.)

We have *our* crew—our own duo. Our double-wedding/next-door-neighbors/our-grandkids-will-marry-each-other FOREVER friendship.

Plus, I haven't joined an organized activity since I was eight. My dance teacher told my mom he felt bad taking any more of her money because after two years, I still couldn't twirl. *Twirl*, Olivia.

I did look up LARPing. Just for fun. It means live-action role-playing. Like you pretend you're a warrior from some video or card game. I was trying to think of something I'm really into, like a comic book character, but the only thing I'm really a fangirl about is *Love and Deception*. Oh, and Rice

Krispies Treats! Maybe I can dress like one of those guys on the cereal box? Snap? No, Crackle.

Okay. Now I have to say it.

I feel better now.

It's so pretty out today. I love that about where we live in California. You know you're either going to get sunny, a few cloudy wisps, or a sprinkle of rain, but not forever rain. And *never* snow. Olivia, there are people out there who have to deal with snow! Think of all the time it must take to put on snow boots and shovel out of your doorway. And they probably never really warm up and can't wear flip-flops in October. Those poor kids.

My mom needed to stop by the stationery store today while Luke was at volleyball. It turned out this huge Christmas order came in, and she had to look through inventory right away, even though Christmas is two months away! So I took the twins across the street to Crazy Tre's Ice Cream—the one with the new disco ball over the counter. Then we walked over to Dad's Mr. Brake shop and I gave them a quarter for the candy machine with old M&M's. And then we went and rolled around in the grass square in front of the courthouse, even though Spencer was sticky from the ice cream.

We were laughing about the grass stuck to his cheeks when this guy who had to be in high school stopped on the sidewalk. Yeah, I know, I didn't even freak out, because why would a boy in high school talk to *me*? I figured he needed directions.

"Hey, aren't you Talin Jorgensen's little sister?" he asked.

"Yes! And we are her brothers!" Spencer raised his hand like he was in class.

The guy laughed. "Talin is, like, the prettiest girl in our grade."

"Um, okay," I said. Talin being pretty isn't a newsflash.

"Tell her Corey says hi." He waved at Flynn. Then he said to me, "You don't really look like her at all."

What. Was that. Supposed to mean? Talin is pretty and *I don't look like her*? That Corey guy belongs in Danny's JERK CLUB. They should give him a double membership because he never even asked my name. Should I only introduce myself as Talin's little sister? Join the Sisters of Pretty Girls in America Club?

Speaking of clubs, another club that would be cool would be Star in a TV Show Club, where you cast people in your real life into whatever show you want. Forget *Love and Deception*, my siblings would make a great sitcom.

> TALIN:
> The beautiful social butterfly who has stupid
> boys like Corey liking her.
> LUKE:
> The star athlete and brother who gives high fives
> that almost break your hand.
> FLYNN and SPENCER:
> The adorable comic relief, like the Olsen twins
> on that old show *Full House*.

Have you ever noticed that sometimes they kill off a sibling on those shows? Like it's the third season, and they realize that middle sister who just babysits and knits while watching soaps is kind of boring, so they pretend like she was never in the family?

It's a good thing we aren't a sitcom. I would be bye-bye by third season.

But besides that moment with Carey ... Curry ... Corey ... (see? Already forgot his stupid name), things are good. I woke up this morning, stared at the cup of water by my bed, and thought, "Hey. That glass is half full." (It was actually almost empty, because I wake up all night to drink water and then have to go to the bathroom, but you get the point.) But it felt good to think it was half full.

I like my school and I can knit a mean scarf. My brothers really ARE adorable. My mom made me some snickerdoodles.

I have this notebook.

And you.

I could go on forever, but then I would use everything up before I write my five grateful things.

My point is . . . just because we had this almost-no-classes-together situation happen, it doesn't mean we can't be fine with how things are. You can start bringing books to lunch. Interesting, factual books. Then you can be an expert on unicorns or sharks or unicorn-sharks.

We can hang posters and maybe other people who like unicorn-sharks will sit next to you. You don't need to be friends with them, but they can just be seat fillers until the important characters (like me) can show up. I will read books about demon warriors, and Bethany and her friends will be too scared to sit by me. All I'm trying to say is, it's going to be fine. Not my-life-is-perfect fine, but we-can-survive-it fine. Survive it without having to fling yo-yos in an after-school club. Unless we want to. We can be whatever we want!

Okay, gotta run to science. We're learning about atoms and it's almost as interesting as unicorn-sharks. Almost.

See you tonight at the shelter!

Loves,

Piper

Grateful: SEE ABOVE. And then add unicorn-sharks. Which might just be a narwhal, but I'm okay with that.

Really, who ISN'T okay with a narwhal?

OLIVIA!!!!!!!!!!

We interrupt our regularly scheduled chat with...

⚡ BREAKING ⚡
⚡ NEWS! ⚡

I take back almost everything I said above about being all cool with the way things are. Because! BECAUSE!!! This morning, when my mom was dropping me off at school, she said, "So I've been thinking about your birthday coming up."

"In six weeks and six days," I said. (Who says you're the only math girl?)

"Your dad and I were talking, and I know you usually don't have the most . . . festive of celebrations with a December birthday."

"Last year you put frosting on a fruitcake."

"Well, this year we thought . . . we want to do an extra-special birthday this year. It's your turn to go big. Invite friends."

"You mean besides Olivia?"

"Yes. You can invite twelve friends. Since you're turning twelve. And I know you've been dying to go to that pottery-painting store, and maybe we could go next door to Crown Pizza after."

I actually got dizzy. Like everything-spinning-in-the-middle-of-carpool-lane DIZZY. Because I have never had a birthday party like this. Not ever. When I was eight, a few friends came over to watch *The Little Mermaid* and Mom bought store-made cupcakes. And I guess she tried to do one when I was five, but all the parents had holiday parties they had to attend, so no one really showed. It's bound to happen when you have a December fifteenth birthday in a large family and parents who are big into "not spoiling" and "staying

Shop Doodle Bugs!

humble." Although Mom does make the perfect birthday baskets. Remember those rainbow fluffy socks?

Come to think of it, YOU'VE never even been to my birthday party, since you kind of ARE my birthday party every year. Imagine if there are other people there to celebrate with you! All the friendly enthusiasm doesn't need to rest on you anymore. Although, let's be honest, it's not the friendly enthusiasm I'm after.

It's the scandal. The intrigue. The DRAMA. Birthday parties are my favorite plot device on soap operas! Someone always dies, or kisses an ex, or gets water thrown in their face. The cakes have a million tiers, and there was that time in season six when Trinity Wentworth rented out an entire ballroom and everyone dressed like flappers and we found out that Ronald was really Jasmine's brother!

"Anyway, just think about who you want to invite!" Mom said. "We should probably send invitations out early since it's such a busy time of year."

My ears were ringing. Invite. Invite? If this was going to be the most dramatic event of the season, I would have to INVITE PEOPLE first. List so far:

1. Olivia (woot!)
2. Andrea, my nine-year-old play pal. And Danny better not drop her off, because he is SO not invited.
3. Um, my family? Can I count that as 3 through 7?
4. Ms. Benson? Maybe she can get me an inspirational poster as a gift.
5. Trigger. The Dog.
6. Blinkie. I hope your cat gets along with Trigger. Oh, wait. Cats are one of Trigger's

dislikes on his adoption card. Well, he hasn't met Blinkie!

7. Maybe the girls from my church class. I mean, they would sure bring the drama, and as long as it's not Savannah Swanson Incident drama, I'm for it.

Clearly, we have a problem. I can't have this epic birthday bash if I don't have any friends to invite. Oh! Maybe I can just hire actors. The MORE DRAMATIC, the merrier. Wait! Do you think we can get someone to jump out of the cake? That's cinematic.

I can't tell my parents I don't have guests. They're giving me this amazing party and I have to deliver. I'm already their kid who doesn't DO anything; I can't be their kid who doesn't have enough friends to invite to a birthday.

Pottery Palace has an owl cookie jar that would look so cute in my room. I want that cookie jar like

Cookie Monster wants . . . well . . . you know.

So, what if . . .
We do the clubs.

Hey, listen! I have a great reason. Great reasons.
You: Practice your conversational skills so you can
finally talk to Jackson. Once you've chatted up
strangers while petting a stingray at Sea Club,
saying hi to Jackson in the hallway Will. Be.
Cake. (Birthday cake!) It will probably help those
stomachaches you get too.

Me: Cast my party. I mean, find people to invite
to my party. No, no . . . cast. I will meet a
bunch of people and figure out what roles they
can play. We HAVE to go to French Club. *Love
and Deception*'s third-best villain, Pierre LeFou, is
French!

I'm serious, Olivia. It's win-win for both of us.

PIPER JORGENSEN

Let's get our club on.
Piper

Grateful: Birthday parties, birthday locations,
birthday scandals, birthday invites, and finding
birthday ~~characters~~ guests!

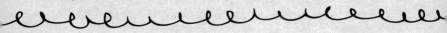

Piper,

Will a forbidden secret be revealed at your Pottery Palace birthday? Or will Cecil Harmond exact revenge on his former love who now has amnesia? Find out next time on . . . Piper's Birthday Party!

This is incredible news! Every bit of it . . . all up until you said "twelve people." So you're right . . . Ms. Benson's idea of hitting up clubs is our only option. You'll find people to cast for your party and I'll practice making conversation. For Jackson. I won't have to rely solely on my writing skills to communicate with him.

But you should probably cut number seven. Anyone associated with Savannah Swanson is someone I CAN'T POSSIBLY create pottery with. Or be friendly with. Or *anything* with.

I have no doubt we can find enough people to cast your party. That's why meeting people at clubs is a brilliant idea.

LET'S DO IT!

Strangely enough, my cup is starting to feel half full.

FULL, Piper!

Now, if you don't mind, I need to get a little planner-y since I get hives if I don't write things down in list form.

OLIVIA & PIPER'S CLUB SCHEDULE-O-RAMA!
(Adding "o-rama" makes it sound more festive, yes?)

☆ MONDAY—Drama (We're probably the definition of drama.)

☆ TUESDAY—Spelling Bee (This might actually be fun. Remember how I totally nailed "believe" in the fourth-grade spelling bee? Knowing "i before e except after c" is practically my superpower.)

☆ WEDNESDAY—LARPing Club (I don't know why I picked this, but it's fun to pronounce.)

☆ THURSDAY—Badminton (This might not be a great decision since the word "bad" is right there in the name. Thoughts?)

☆ FRIDAY—French Club (We could use the practice. Also there might be food.)

*Note: other clubs to consider: LEGO Club, Sea Club, Japanese Animation, Chess Club

**Another note: these are simply suggestions. Your input is welcome. Just know that our schedule is packed already with our pet-shelter volunteering and your mom making you babysit like you're an employee.

Let's talk more tonight at the shelter. Yippee!!!

Girl with a glass half full of pomegranate juice.
(Note to aliens: pomegranate juice is delicious and a
beautiful shade of red.)
Olivia

O—

I can't believe we're stuck in opposite parts of the shelter. AGAIN. At least we can slide this back and forth every time you pass by the office.

I like your schedule. Of course you made a schedule. I will have to check with my mom on babysitting days.

Back to filing. Enjoy the animals. Write back!!

Piper—

I'm bummed we're in the opposite parts of the shelter too! Glad you like the schedule so far. Can we agree to skip the Yo-Yo Club? We all know one of us will end up with an eye injury.

Also, Trigger keeps gnawing on his leash like it's a ribeye. I wish you were out here with me.

O—

I've been thinking about the LARPing one because anyone who goes there is obviously into acting. It's an easy casting call. But also it might be cool to dress up and pretend to be someone else, even if we have no idea who the characters are.

Unless I have to dress up as a dog. Or a cat. Any animal, really. We get enough animal action here.

P—

Let's follow the schedule next week and see if our lives turn around completely. That's not asking too much of an after-school activity, is it?

We'll start with Spelling Bee Club!

O—

What kind of people spell fOR FuN? Unless they get all their boring out in spelling club and are really wild at lunchtime? Never mind, as long as they can spell P-A-R-T-Y they are okay with me. Are you going to spell I-L-I-K-E-Y-O-U to Jackson?

I bet spellers are good at reading scripts and enunciating their lines.

You know, some days I don't notice the smell here. Today is not that day.

EWW

P—

I'm looking at the options not on the schedule and I'm guessing we should cross off LEGO Club because of that injury you got when you stepped on your little brother's Luke Skywalker.

O—

That light saber . . . ow! I just had a phantom foot pain. I can do LEGO Club if I wear very thick boots. Wait, isn't Jackson in LEGO Club? He wrote a comment on Bethany's blog.

P—

WHAT? Jackson's in the LEGO Club?! How did I miss that? Forget your foot injury, let's go! The schedule says LEGO Club is next Monday at 3:30. We will erase Drama Club. That still gives us time to make it to the shelter. This is the perfect answer. . . . I'll meet new people this week and get some charming conversational skills in time for LEGO Club! Jackson Whittaker will fall in love with my ability to form complete sentences!

O—

Maybe we want to do a couple of weeks of clubs so you can REALLY get prepared for LEGO Club? But not too many weeks, since Thanksgiving is the last week of November, and I should probably have my guest list before then. I'll have to get invitations out a couple weeks early since December fifteenth is, seriously, the worst day ever to be born ever besides December sixteenth to twenty-fifth.

Not that this is totally about my birthday. It's about you! Romance! Jackson Whittaker! I got it.

P—

Is it weird that I am doing all this just so I can learn to . . . talk to a *guy*?

O—

I'm hoping my life will LITERALLY become a soap opera. You're asking the wrong person.

I need to check this schedule with my mom because of babysitting. I think half of the reason she works is for the easy access to supplies for her famous gift baskets. But the other half is so she can have a break from the twins, a reason to shower, and to not wear those used-to-be-black yoga pants every day.

P—

As long as they are LONG yoga pants, I think it's a solid uniform.

So we are good with Spelling Club, LARPing, and LEGO. I was going to add Chess Club, but maybe not. Dad finally sat down with me last night to play a game but he got called away for work. Honestly, the thought of playing without him makes my insides ache.

Okay, gotta go give Trigger a talking to. He started digging a hole and may reach a water pipe soon.

O—

Totally, no thanks on Chess Club. That one time you tried to explain it to me, I almost died from boredom.

My mom is here. Leaving the notebook with you. I'm actually excited! I think this is really going to work for *both* of us. Good thing, too, since my birthday is only a month and a half away! Tick, tock.

Also, I know we agreed that last year would be the LAST year we dressed up for Halloween, but my mom asked me to take the twins around, so if you want to come trick-or-treating, let me know. You can dress up like Amelia Earhart again and I'll dress up as Tatiana Vickers—the cruel and sophisticated socialite on *Love and Deception* who owns her own fashion empire and is secretly dying of a rare disease.

The twins are dressing as Dr. Seuss THING 1 and THING 2. The costume options for twins are endless.

Call me tonight and we'll plan clubs *and* Halloween costumes. Or wait—I'll call you, once I can hide in the bathroom from all the rug rats. What is it like to have your own room?

See you tomorrow at Spelling Bee Club. Let's hope they're party people.

Welcome
to the
SPELLING BEE CLUB . . .
where you can bee amazing!!

Learn new fabulous words!

Work with your friends to become
a better speller!

Eat yummy snacks!

BEE HAPPY!

Piper,

This flyer was a bit misleading, right? I pictured the two of us walking into a room full of gleeful people snacking on gourmet pastries as they spelled words like MAGNIFICENT. And REGALEMENT.

But no. Desk work? Silent study? I didn't actually want to spell words, I wanted to CHAT with people about spelling words. I really don't mind worksheets, but in my free time? That one exercise where we had to spell out a word three times before the timer went off almost gave me a panic attack. I only got through two spellings of the word *platitudinous* before my timer buzzed and I jumped. And I noticed you almost fell out of your chair. I wanted to hug you, but the teacher slapped another worksheet on my desk.

Anyhow, while you were in the bathroom, I walked back to the snack table next to Mia Lester—that girl who always wears that Pokémon sweatshirt with the worn-off glitter. She didn't even wait for me to attempt a charming comment, she just went on about how excited she is that we have snacks this year because apparently last year they didn't have any money in the budget and there were financial issues and they needed to increase their donations and she said it all in one long sentence and all without taking a breath.

So I nodded in agreement.

ITWASAWESOME.

But those snacks? Goldfish crackers and tap water. What are we . . . toddlers? I gave Mia a donation of five dollars and she said thank you. I don't think that makes her a "friend" or anything, but it was cool.

How'd you do? I did notice that you asked the teacher four separate times if you could go to the bathroom. Hope you're okay.

Hugs,

Olivia

Grateful for:

1. Other chances via practice clubs that will (hopefully) help me get ready to be fabulous at LEGO Club!

2. The fact that I actually CAN spell *platitudinous*

3. The homemade cornbread my mom made me last night (cornbread and sweet potato pie remind her of

Sunday dinners in Atlaaaaanta.)

4. That assembly earlier today that got me out of PE

5. My eight-year-old neighbor who let me borrow his LEGOs so I could practice before the club—small, boxy houses with one window . . . Here I come!

O—

These are the three words I remember from the list: "chivalry,"
"facsimile," "tendetius" (or maybe it was "tetnus"?). I don't
know if I'm spelling them right—I'm sure I'm not. But I don't
care. We both know I was never going to be a spelling bee
winner, or a spelling bee participant, or a spelling bee anything. The very idea is perposterous. Preposterous? Silly.

Although, I will say, I didn't feel like a complete idiot in
there. The thing I like about middle school is only a few people remember me as the Girl Who Used to Get Humiliated If
She Had to Contribute in Reading Group. Middle school is a
fresh start. And I think, I THINK, I'm beginning to understand some more in reading classes now. Maybe it's all this
writing and reading we do in our notebook? I don't know.
Don't tell anyone. You know how Mom has me going to this
tutor now one day a week during lunch? Well, she always puts
homemade peanut butter cups in my lunch that day. I don't
want to lose *that*.

So the reason I went to the bathroom four times was not just to escape silent *P*s and weird vowel combinations.

First of all, we had a Medieval Day in English class today. We were combined with a seventh grade class. Lemonade Stand Danny's seventh grade class. So he cornered me when I was sampling the carbonated apple juice "ale."

Here's the script.

[*Interior, daytime*]

DANNY: Hey, wench.

ME: I'm not a wrench.

DANNY (*guffaws*): Wench. Not wrench. Duh.

ME: Oh, that's right. 'Cuz *you're* the tool. (I really said that! I'm not sure what tool means, but I know it's not good, and he seemed mad, so it worked.)

DANNY (*shoves a tart into his mouth*): How come you aren't wearing your glasses?

ME (*a little weirded out that he noticed*): I have contacts, but sometimes I get allergies and they bother my eyes. And sometimes I just like to accessorize.

DANNY: Cool. So . . . I saw you at lunch today sitting with that girl Tessa.

ME (*tries to recover from the shock of Danny noticing me at*

school, and that he thinks I really hang out with Tessa. I'm not
trying to be friends with those girls, Olivia. You KNOW that.):
Yeah. So?

DANNY: So I think she's cute. Can you tell her?

ME: You like Tessa?

DANNY: That's what I just said. I know you're just a sixth
grader, so you probably don't understand how this works.

ME: Sure I do. I tell her you think she's cute. And then
you do something nice for me.

DANNY (*crosses arms*): Fine. Like what?

ME: I'm not sure yet. Maybe bow down in the cafeteria?
Or wash our driveway. Oh, or let me run a truck over your
lemonade stand. The fun part is thinking about it for a while.
(Olivia, maybe I can borrow some of Danny's not-as-mean
friends for my birthday party? They could be the villains and
wear fedoras. Every party should have a fedora.)

DANNY: She's in after-school orchestra with me. If you
can tell her before that, and let me know if she likes me back,
then I can ask her out afterward. Deal?

ME (*flicks hair. Because aren't you supposed to do that when
you talk to boys? Should we add that to your Jackson ideas?*):
You know, if you want something from a girl, you shouldn't
call her a wench.

DANNY (*swigs his ale and burps. Gross.*): Fine. Thanks.

ME: You're welcome, Village Idiot.

[*End Scene*]

So then I ate some tarts and meat pie. I also went a little crazy on the ale, which is why I left Spelling Bee Club the first time—I had to go the bathroom.

The second time I left was to pull Tessa out of orchestra with a fake note so I could tell her Danny likes her.

And guess what? She likes him. Lemonade-selling, wears-stupid-shirts-that-say-funny-things-that-aren't-funny, rude, brown-eyed, messy-haired Danny. She actually likes him. So THEN Danny met up with me on the third bathroom break and I told him the news. I guess they'll go out now. I still don't quite know what going out means? Maybe they will hold hands in the hallway or something. La-dee-da.

And fourth break—I truly had to go to the bathroom again.

Anyway, although Spelling Bee Club was absolutely a bust, the kids in there seemed nice. A couple of girls smiled at me while I ate Goldfish. But I'm not sure I should consider them as birthday party people. They can spell "scandal," but I have to figure out if they can actually *create* it.

Which reminds me. I'm working on my birthday party ROLES. I'll add it to the notebook.

<3

Piper

Grateful: that no guys are "asking me out" since I still don't know what that means, apple ale, knowing how to spell some words, Medieval Day, adventure!

P.S. Oh my gosh, what if we taught Blinkie how to spell just by BLINKING? Now that would be an online video worth watching. . . .

Piper's Birthday of Intrigue, Drama and . . .

SCANDAL!!!

Cast of characters:

ASHLEY DESDEMONA: Our heroine! Strong and spunky! Wears beautiful scarves and fashionable eyewear! Can do a fierce round kick and save a baby from a fire! Sometimes has money problems! Played by me, obviously.

RANDALL MENARD: Super villain. If you took all the villains in the galaxy and added them together, they still would not reach his level of EVIL. Some of Randall's notorious villainous acts include blackmail, secretly having a family in another country, faking a ghost haunting, and holding BIG glamorous parties where someone is always murdered when the lights go out. Silver hair. Hasn't aged in fifty years. Played by Danny, if I invited him, which I'm not going to do.

TATIANA VICKERS: The cruel and sophisticated social-ite who owns her own fashion empire and is secretly dying of a rare disease. Evil, but sympathetic. Wears a lot of rings. Her skin looks frozen. Talin? Her face doesn't look frozen, but she's *très* (French!) fashionable.

MCKAY DAVIS: This guy has a jaw so cut, he can sell razors without even doing a commercial. Even though he's done loads of commercials. Classically handsome, incredibly kind. He had Inconsistent Blindness for two seasons, a condition where people just become blind every once in a while for no reason. Very tragic. Luke, my ridiculously athletic brother? Or maybe I won't need to cast relatives at all with all the people I'm meeting at the clubs!

CECIL HARMOND: Has had more boyfriends than anyone can count. She is always trying to get back at an ex. She also has a lovely garden and makes grilled cheese whenever there is a cozy scene with lots of explaining. Played by Olivia, to get her used to the idea of having a boyfriend?

Just the first names of common characters who would need to be replicated in the birthday party:

JOSEPH—a twin (the good one who can cry on a dime)

JOSEF—the other twin (evil) (has been married A LOT) (never cries). The twins? Except either one could start crying over anything at any moment. And they're three.

LASHELLE—constantly gets stranded in snowstorms with no access to a phone, only a cute guy and a fireplace

DAMIAN—has multiple personalities; embarrasses the family at Christmas

BERNARD—was deaf but has been miraculously cured!

HEATHER—returns from the dead ALL THE TIME

Stock roles that can be played by anyone:

A BUTLER—a twin?

A BARTENDER—twin? But potential spills.

A nanny

A doctor with bad news

A person who answers the phone at the police station and is always annoyed

Also, my mom said the other day she's worried I watch too much *Love and Deception* and should maybe go kick a soccer ball sometime. Hahahaha, right?

Thanks for shopping at CVS!

CA sales tax: 8.00%
Cashier: Sandy M.

1	Sterile gauze pads	$5.99
1	Twenty-five adhesive bandages (assorted sizes)	$4.99
1	Athletic tape _(!)_	$3.99
1	Reusable cold pack with adjustable strap	$17.99
1	Frozen foot-pain relief	$9.99
1	Hydrocortisone ointment	$6.99
2	Kit Kat candy bars	$1.49

8 ITEMS

_one dark chocolate for me,
milk chocolate for you_

SUBTOTAL	$51.43
TAX	$4.12
TOTAL	$55.55
CASH	$60.00
CHANGE	$4.45

_I'll explain the need for all
the first-aid supplies . . .
so embarrassing._

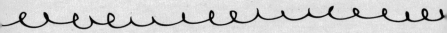

Piper,

No, my dad does not hoard first-aid supplies. Let me explain:

I decided to go check out Badminton Club, even though you ended up not being able to go. Aren't you proud of me? By myself! It required LOTS of deep, cleansing breaths.

But truthfully, I wish your mom could find a babysitter for the twins from an outside source. They can't play every role in your DRAMATIC party, no matter how cute they are. We need guests! (Thanks for giving me the part of someone with an embarrassment of boyfriends!)

So, club time. There was a poster on the gym wall that said: "Badminton is more than just a birdie and a racket! It's a place to build friendships!"

"Building friendships" is fairly close to "getting charming conversational skills to use on a guy."

Perfection, right?

Let me start off by saying that I'm writing this in bed with my knee elevated while I'm balancing an ice pack on it. I'm on my third ice pack, so don't hold me accountable for the words I'm about to say.

The Badminton Club's idea of "building friendships" is to pair us off and hit the birdie back and forth with a partner. The pair next to us talked and giggled the whole way through. But MY partner happened to be this girl from my history class, Jessica Belfort. She talks incessantly during class. She talks to her friends. To strangers. To her textbook. The girl is A TALKER, is what I'm saying. So I was feeling good that she was my partner—someone to talk to!

However.

It just so happened that Jessica had two teeth pulled earlier that day and her mouth was full of cotton balls. She couldn't say a word. All she did was moan.

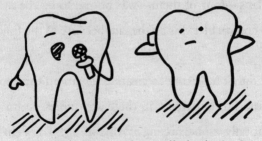

Jessica moaned out all the lyrics
to a sad Taylor Swift song

It wasn't all that bad, since we communicated through eyebrow raises. I now have specific eyebrow positions for "it's my serve," "good hit," and "I like your boots." Pretty cool, actually. Hopefully Jackson will fall for my eyebrow gestures?

But truthfully, I was hoping we'd rotate partners so I could attempt to hold a conversation with someone—a person with a voice—but that's when the exercise portion of the club kicked in. . . .

Mrs. Rodriguez blew her whistle. "Four laps. No stopping. You can't play competitive badminton if you're out of shape."

As you know, lap running is not something I do—or have ever done, actually. I'm certain that if I started doing it I would instantly get woozy and possibly die. I know this because the simple act of jogging up my street to catch the school bus has caused me to see a white light on more than one occasion. So running laps—four of them—was bound to be the death of me. But I couldn't let this be the end because of the following reasons:

1. I didn't have time to clean up my room this morning and I'm fairly certain there are undies on my floor. Totally embarrassing if an FBI agent had to come search my room due to my suspicious death. Very soap opera-y, right? (Wait. Does the FBI come by if you die playing badminton? Hold on . . . okay, I'm back. Google says probably not.)

2. I still have LEGO Club to look forward to next week.

I'll never become the future Mrs. Whittaker if I never get a chance to talk to Jackson and/or I'm super dead.

So anyway, I tried to negotiate with Mrs. Rodriguez. "How about two really good laps?"

She squinted at me and tried to stare down into my soul. "This is competitive badminton. Four laps, no less."

I bit at my lip, scared to correct her. "But I'm fairly sure this is a 'club.'" (I even used the air quotes when I said it.) "Can't we just play for 'fun'?" (I air-quoted 'fun' too. What is wrong with me?)

By the look on her face, I could tell she wasn't just staring at my soul . . . she was being all judgy with it. "We take this seriously. It's fun in a serious, competitive way. Now run!"

I didn't see a choice, so I started my laps around the gym. The first lap was almost enjoyable. The second lap was mildly intolerable. By the third lap I got completely bored, and that's when it all fell apart. "Fell" is the key word in that sentence.

My mind started wandering back to years earlier, when my brother started middle school. There was a school orientation and they held the meeting right here in this gym. I remember sitting in the bleachers in between my parents and feeling very small. I was only six years old, so that makes sense.

Mom adjusted the red-and-black bows in my hair (the colors of the University of Georgia Bulldogs) and she squeezed my hand as we watched Jason walk up to get his sixth grade orientation packet. But what I remember most was the look on Dad's face as he watched Jason.

Pride. So much pride.

It was the same exact look he had on his face a few months ago when we sat in the bleachers at Stanford, watching Jason at his college orientation.

Dad looking very proud.

Mom squeezing my hand.

And me, sitting in the bleachers, feeling very small.

Bleachers. With all my daydreaming, I didn't even notice that they were pulled out slightly, and on that third lap—without warning—my foot caught the corner of the bottom bleacher and I tripped.

But it wasn't just a simple tripping. Wham! I wiped out on the hardwood floor.

I banged up my toe, knee, shoulder, hand, and even my ear. MY EAR, Piper. All I could think about was how much I wanted to be at home letting Mom take care of me.

Mrs. Rodriguez let me call home so I could be picked up early, but not before she leaned in and whispered, "I don't think competitive badminton is your thing, Olivia. Try Drama Club."

Mom wasn't home.

Talk about feeling alone in the world. I know you say you feel ignored at your house too, but my feeling ignored means NO ONE IS AROUND. It's not the same. Sorry for my sudden whiny moment, but I just want to remind you how lucky you are.

Anyway, I had no choice—with my knee beginning to throb and my little toe aching—I had to call Dad at work.

He left work early and picked me up and surprisingly he didn't even complain about it. CVS was having a sale on first-aid items so I hobbled around and grabbed everything I needed, plus a couple more items just in case I have another falling-while-attempting-to-make-conversation incident.

And get this. Sandy, the cashier at the CVS, was super chatty! I told her all about my injuries and she told me about all their sales and some of their new products. They have a new self-tanner in stock now. It wasn't a conversation with another student, but it was a conversation.

It was progress.

It's possible we could invite her to the birthday party if we need someone to play the role of Helpful Cashier with a Kind Smile.

Dad took me home, put the ice pack in the fridge, "buddy taped" my hurt toe to the next toe over, poured me some hot tea, and watched some of season four of *Gilmore Girls* with me. I leaned on his shoulder and he scratched my head. It was the first time we'd hung out like that in a really long time. It was . . . amazing.

I'll be honest, I kind of wanted it to last forever.

You would think now that Jason is gone, I'd be smothered with Mom's and Dad's attention. But, no. It took full-body injuries to get Dad to watch TV with me.

So now here I am, in bed, thinking over tomorrow. Dad wants me to stay home so he can monitor this toe, which is swollen and may be sprained, and also this bruise, which is as big as my palm. I've never gotten a sprain or a bruise from a social situation before. And you know what? It's awesome! It makes me feel like an interesting person.

So you'll have to do LARP tomorrow by yourself, sorry. Of course, I'll call you once this throbbing dies down. Dad said he would drop the notebook on your doorstep in the morning with the Kit Kat.

Even though I didn't chat up (I love that expression. So British.) many people today, I still have a bruise—an amazing one—that I can use for a conversation starter. Who's looking on the bright side now?

But I'm thinking let's stay away from any other clubs involving the word "competitive."

"Olivia"

Grateful for:

1. Chatty cashiers at CVS
2. Kit Kats
3. That we still have some club choices left
4. The SpongeBob Band-Aids because they're just so cute
5. A dad who knows exactly how I like my head to be scratched

P.S.!! Get me your notes on my notes to that note to Jackson.

PIPER JORGENSEN

great start

Hey, Jackson,

Since you are new in our math class, I thought I would send you a friendly letter with pointers on how to survive period 3. Just helping out another classmate.

1. Don't even think about getting your cell phone out. (Larry Higgins) had his taken away two weeks ago and still hasn't gotten it back.

2. ADD SOMETHING SMART HERE, LIV. I don't even know what you study in math. Half the kids in my class can't even multiply fractions. (Yes. I'm in that half. It's not worth it to me to deal with any number less than one.)

3. The pencil sharpener in this room is like a ferochius shark. It gobbles up pencils. If you need anything sharpened, come see me. (BTW, did I spell ferochius right?)

Act like you don't know he'll be in there. Like... "And if math really isn't your thing, you should totally check out this fun club I just joined—Extreme LEGOs. Things get extreme in there. We're talking ships and architectural wonders. I mean, if you're into LEGOs. Are you?"

Margin notes:

Cute is fine. Wowzers... not so much. Flirt it up here.

I have no idea what you are talking about. This sounds about right to me. You are trying to hook him with your smartness—show it off.

Or should this opener be more flirty? We could use words like "cute," and "lol, and "wowzers!"

Also, Larry Higgins will only wear shirts that are the color green. Not that it has anything to do with the topic at hand, but it's something I've noticed.

Smart? Okay, got it: I know all about equations if you need help. My favorite ones are linear equations that are basic polynomials with a degree of one. And now I sound like A GIANT NERD. (Help. Me.)

Don't mention the Larry Higgins-green shirt observation. In a note to a boy you want to avoid TOO many tangents. Stay focused. It's like in a soap opera—you can have a car crash or a long-lost brother, but not in the same episode.

Okay, I think you already covered your smarts above, so maybe now we mention LEGO Club?

No, you didn't spell it right, but your effort is adorable.

Again. One car crash. Leave out the long-lost brother.

PIPER JORGENSEN

And once he smelled like black olives. Not sure if that's important, but wanted to point it out.

Baby steps. Speak a full sentence to him first. Then we can discuss visitations.

4. Yes, Mr. Dreadmore does smell like breakfast sausage. But sometimes he smells like syrup too, so those even out.

I don't know if you have any pets, but I work at an animal shelter once a week and we get all sorts of cool creatures coming in there. You should stop by the shelter for a visit.

Should I talk about creatures here? Boys like things that are gross and predator-ish, right? Yep.

Dinosaurs. Grizzly bears. Mutant turtles. All that.

Piper! What if he actually DID come by sometime?

I'm hyperventilating. Jackson Whittaker . . . VISITING ME. Deep, cleansing breath, deep, cleansing breath

Maybe you'd like to sit at lunch together sometime. You might like it. I suspect we are soulmates.

Instead of saying "soulmates" maybe I should just draw some hearts? I don't want him getting a restraining order. Oh! I could draw an anatomically correct heart, like the ones they put in science books. That way, he won't know if I'm hinting at love or just really good at organ illustrations. He'd think . . . he'd wonder . . . HE'D FALL FOR ME. That, or get nauseous.

Well, write back if you get a chance. And put that cell phone away, you crazy kid!

*cough, restraining order, *cough

~~I'm obsessed with you,~~

Olivia

Right?! perfect ending

Whatever. I still like this line. But if you don't, maybe mention LEGO Club again. If you pass this to him before that, it will be a good icebreaker.

Again, SARCASM. Try it. But seriously, a heart might not be a bad idea. Guys are all a little bit gross. My brothers and Danny have shown me that. And you're really good at drawing all that scientific stuff, so go with what you're good at.

From:loveanddeceptionfan@gmail.com

To: westonfamily706@yahoo.com

Subject: Piper gets her LARP on!

Ah-live-ee-ahhhh,

I'm saying your name like that because I'm trying to work on enunciating. Sorry. Eee-nun-cee-ate-ing. It's a LARP thing.

How is Da Bruise? (That's its name now. You have no say about this.) I'm sorry that it's grown so big—that picture you sent me was nasty. And I'm sorry you had to waste time at the doctor's office doing X-rays instead of watching more *Gilmore Girls*. Especially since their prognostics (prognosis? recommendation?) was to elevate your leg. Which is something you could do at home. In bed. Watching TV.

I'm sending you this email because there is no way I can get you the notebook tonight. Since your parents ~~are crazy protective~~ love you very much, and you have a family email account, your mom or dad might be reading this. Hello, Mr. and/or Mrs. Weston! Ignore any mention of a boy named Jackson (your daughter's soulmate). And when I say "notebook," I just mean French homework. Don't worry about that.

Back to MY family. This was the whiteboard schedule for the Jorgensens for today:

12:30 Pick up twins from preschool

1:30 Gymnastics for Flynn and Spencer

3:00 School carpool

3:30 Piper LARP Club (I made the whiteboard. Woot!)

3:30 Talin Student Council

3:45 Luke coach's meeting

4:00 Neighborhood-watch meeting

4:45 Talin violin

5:00 Flynn dentist!

6:30 Luke Boy Scouts

7:00 Drop off dinner for Andersons

Mom was so busy that she made the Andersons OUR dinner and we ate McDonald's in the car. The twins got into a French fry war, and I'm sure we'll find fossilized potatoes in the minivan seats for months now. Maybe your dad can study old fast food for anthropology. (Hey, look at me, spelling *anthropology* I'm pretty sure correctly.)

Looking at a regular old day, you can see that there is nothing on the schedule for things like watching *Gilmore*

Girls, at least not with one of my parents. I don't think I've ever watched an episode of TV with my dad. Is that weird? We've gone fishing a few times, usually with Luke and Talin. I mean, I love my parents, and they love me, but there's never much one-on-one bonding.

Most of the time, I'm glad about that. I like doing my own thing whenever and wherever I want (when not on twin duty). But other times, I totally understand what you're saying. There are different ways to feel alone. Trust me, alone can happen in the middle of busy. Alone can be the best feeling, but it can also be the worst.

But that's not why I'm writing. You want to hear all about Live-Action Role-Playing—LARP Club. You might be disappointed that today's adventure did not include people dressed up like mutant lizards with weapons. That's *combat* LARP, and this group voted last month that they would focus the semester on *theater-style* LARP. Yes, there are different kinds of LARP. And I didn't even know LARP existed until we started this club thing. Also, LARP is the worst word to say over and over again. Try it! LARP, LARP, LARP, LARP . . .

Sorry, now you can't stop saying it, can you?

So there I was, all ready to smoosh Orcs with a foam sword, and instead I was given the attached sheet for my "character." And we did this whole murder mystery where we were at some heiress's wedding on a remote island. I was assigned the Cat Lady, who dies in the first five minutes, because I'm new.

There wasn't a script. We just got our character info and the Game Master (aka Mr. Gupta) presented scenarios and we went from there. But here's how the story started. To give you an idea. And as you can see, it took me a while to understand how the staying-in-character part works.

GAME MASTER: You are exclusive guests at the Vanderbeens' secret wedding. For reasons unknown, the pilot flew away after the ceremony. You don't know if or when he will return. Do you still hold the wedding reception, or call for help? Begin.

BRIDE (FELICITY) (*wails*): Why is he ruining my wedding day! This is my special day! MINE!

CAT LADY (*Me. I know, I finally do something outside of the animal shelter and it still involves felines!*): And you also brought special people here too, special people who seem like they aren't connected, but they mysteriously are. Sorry, Mr. Gupta, was that too much foreshadowing?

GAME MASTER: Don't break character, Cat Lady. And call me Game Master.

CAT LADY: Sorry. Uh . . . oh, I miss my cats. I hope I see them again!

BRIDE (*stepping in front of me, like we're on an actual stage and she's trying to block me*): Oh, woe is me! I am the star and my dreams are shattered.

The rest of the LARPers sat there for a little bit, seeing who was going to talk next. I was about to tell the bride about the time my cats got fake married, or this other time when a neighbor's vengeful cat tried to murder her mother-in-law . . . but then the groom spoke.

GROOM: I'm sorry. You're pretty. Let's go eat cake.

Then they pretended like they were eating cake. They didn't even really chew that much.

DOCTOR DIPPY *(played by another guy I don't know. This club was filled with guys I don't know. Isn't it funny how many people we don't know at our school, people who may make GREAT party guests?)*: I hope we aren't here for too long. I have surgery tomorrow. I'm putting a monkey brain in a baby.

MILES FLEMING, FAMOUS DIRECTOR: And my new movie starts production this week! Angelina has a very small window to film because she is having a baby.

ME: I really, really miss my cats. . . . Hey, what if Doctor Dippy took out the monkey brain and put it in the groom? That would be kind of funny, right? Hey, groom. Pretend like you're a monkey, then admit you're also the son of a billionaire oil tycoon who—

GAME MASTER: Piper . . . Cat Lady. You need to let the role-players create their own characters. You focus on you.

It went longer, of course. And guess what? I loved it! Who'd have thought? The actual role-playing wasn't the fun part. I liked writing the script more. And directing is so me. It made me incredibly excited to get the cast set for my own birthday! If I was Game Master, things would have been bananas.

I want to host my own LARP sometime and use some of my subplots from playing Barbies with Andrea . . . I mean, *babysitting* Andrea. I should start adding brain surgery into my bag of ideas. Also monkeys.

The only UN-fun part was when the grouchy Game Master said Cat Lady had been eaten by a polar bear. Where'd the polar bear suddenly come from? And how did a polar bear get on a tropical island anyway? So many plot holes.

The problem with casting birthday party guests at LARP is that we weren't allowed to talk to anyone out of character. But I did get a chance to talk to the bride, Felicity, for a little bit after. And I think you'll agree the convo equals total success. . . .

ME: Wow, you're really good at crying on cue.

FELICITY: Thanks! I stare in my mirror for hours and think of sad things and it helps.

ME: Seriously? That's so cool.

FELICITY: I totally liked your coma idea. If LARPing doesn't work out, you should think about being a director.

ME: Do you ever do any acting outside of LARP?

FELICITY: Tons. Drama Club is amazing too. You should come!

ME: What about . . . a life-situation kind of LARP? Like if I had a birthday party, and wanted you to pretend to be someone else the whole time.

FELICITY (*tilts her head*): Like . . . a birthday clown?

ME: Or a tragic heroine who is down on her luck but about to write an amazing *New York Times* best-selling novel. And also has an evil twin?

FELICITY: Sure. I guess. There are no small parts, just small actors.

SO FELICITY IS IN!

Ugh, I'm such a McChatterson! So anyway, LARPing was awesome. And if Felicity doesn't end up making the cut, maybe she's someone we could be friends with—if we ever want another friend.

But I'm okay if that "if" never happens.

Tomorrow! French Club! Which means . . . *MACARONS*!! (Or croissants. Or even baguettes. I will be happy with any pastry.)

Piper

Grateful for: Da Bruise (not the actual bruise, just the name I came up for it), retelling events to you like it's a movie, *macarons*, Flynn being potty-trained, the way the name Felicity feels when you say it. Try it. Fill-is-it-eee.

From: westonfamily706@yahoo.com

To: loveanddeceptionfan@gmail.com

Subject: Re: Piper gets her LARP on!

Piper,

Don't worry about my parents reading our emails. I know they did this whole family email account because they took a class on Protecting Your Child in a Modern World, but they're both so busy that they never log in.

I love that you pretended to be a Cat Lady . . . all to cast your birthday party attenders. YOU'RE MY HERO. I'm so impressed you stayed in there and totally committed to that role.

I'm not going to make it to another club tomorrow because I'm going to stay out of school one more day. No, my bruise and toe sprain aren't THAT much of a medical emergency, but Dad wants to keep an eye on them.

Not seeing you again at school is downright depressing, but get this! Dad and I are going to spend the entire day together having a movie marathon and playing chess games where he will—without a doubt—beat me. I've never won a game against him.

I'll give you a report on how it goes tomorrow by email since you are still the Keeper of the Notebook.

From: westonfamily706@yahoo.com

To: loveanddeception@gmail.com

Subject: Olivia's Day Off

As predicted, my dad beat me every chess game.

I get the feeling he wishes I would win, but I just get so overwhelmed by the bishop that I can't seem to figure out how to get myself out of a jam.

"It's a metaphor for life," Dad said after I lost for the third time. "You use your primitive instinct to methodically build a position, then you analyze your opponent and move in for the kill."

Mom rolled her eyes. "You mean *the win*. Speaking of wins . . ." She was in the middle of finishing the buttercream decoration on her football-shaped Rice Krispies Treats.

The "big game" is this Saturday and the house is already covered in University of Georgia decorations: red-and-black streamers, cups, plates, balloons, and several banners that say, "HOW 'BOUT THEM DAWGS!" Jason used to help her decorate because he loves any football game.

But she didn't need much help this time because it was only the Clemson game. When they play Florida, she goes full-throttle with the party favors and she practically shudders with excitement as she spins around the house getting ready.

Mom's enthusiasm for Georgia football is equal to her enthusiasm for asking prying questions about my life. Her pep about life in general is sort of exhausting sometimes. I *want* to tell her about my life . . . I just wish it would happen in some cool, dramatic moment, like in the movies. Eye contact . . . knowing glances . . . a hand squeeze . . . and then me spilling my heart. You know, movie material. It's not as satisfying to answer a series of questions when she asks them with the same amount of excitement that she uses when questioning the waiter about ingredients in the sweet potato casserole. (She's very particular about casseroles.)

Today Mom wore her "regular" bulldog earrings, but on Florida game day she wears her special silver bulldogs. She had them made—special order—by our local jeweler. "Because our rivalry with those Gators is so huge, it requires *sterling* silver," Mom always says. (Note to aliens—I know this doesn't make a lot of sense. Just go with it. That's my strategy.)

I tasted Mom's football Rice Krispies Treat. "Awwfum!" I said, giving her a thumbs-up. Tasting her party food is really the only interaction I have with her on game days, since I know exactly zero-point-zero about football. Dad doesn't know anything about it either. Which I totally love about him.

We sat down to dinner and Mom was still wearing her apron with the big *G* on it. Dad made an attempt to get this whole football fascination of hers. "You know, the Romans used to arm gladiators for the entertainment of the audience. So I can understand the appeal."

"Football isn't just entertainment." She passed a casserole around and winked at me. "It's an institution."

I had no idea what she meant, and sometimes it feels like none of us understand each other. It's like we're orbiting each other, but we're all on different planets.

So there we sat.

Dad with his newspaper.

Mom with her bulldog earrings.

And me with a sprained toe I got from trying to practice conversation, something I was failing at with my OWN FAMILY.

Jason seemed to be the glue that pulled us all together. Now that he's not home, my parents talk mostly about him, and I don't talk much at all. Mom's latest concern is his eating habits at college. Is he only eating Top Ramen? Is he getting enough vitamin C? They discuss this *every night.* Like I said, the three of us are missing our glue.

But man, that casserole was good . . . loads of fried onions. Maybe casserole can be our new glue?

What do you guys talk about at dinner? I mean, when you all are around to sit down and eat. I still think you have the numbers in your favor when it comes to aloneness. The twins are by your side constantly, and they are so cute. And they need you. Isn't it great that your family NEEDS you?

Anyway, I hope when you went to French Club today it ended up having lots of castable members—and people for me to practice the art of conversation with.

I'm putting together a plan for how to approach Jackson when I see him at LEGO Club. I call it "My Plan of Attack." Too aggressive?

My optional title is the 2-3-73 Plan.

I figure if I say TWO intriguing things . . .

Followed by THREE flirty gestures . . .

The odds of him realizing that I actually LIKE HIM will run at about seventy-three percent.

I don't have any actual math to back that up—it's just more of a hunch. Anyway, those are my working titles. I will create some flowcharts to plan this out in greater detail. Planning ahead is one of my few strengths.

See you soon (bruiseless and with a pinkie toe that works),
Olivia

Grateful for:
   1.   The visual of that guy in LARP actually saying the

words "I'm putting a monkey brain in a baby"

2. The fact that medicine has advanced so much that putting a monkey brain in a baby is probably possible (though not all that practical for the baby)

3. That my bruise is still visible so I have a conversation starter if needed

4. YouTube videos that teach you how to become a better chess player

5. That casserole Mom made

Olivia (did you know that's a French name? Oui?),

We need a rule. No missing school two days in a row. You think one class together isn't a big deal, but that one class is the best part of the day. And after the second day of not having someone to share details with, not having someone to meet with during locker breaks, you start to feel a little sad faced. ☹

And by you, I mean me. Because YOU, Olivia, were home today and I was in class.

Anyway, I was ☹. You are my favorite person, and I wanted to see you. But the good news is, it's Friday and hopefully you are recovered enough this weekend that we can get together. We absolutely MUST strategize, since LEGO Club is on Monday. I'm actually a little nervous for you. Not that you should be nervous.

I mentioned LARP to my parents and my dad said, "Oh, that's perfect for you, Pipe."

And I was, like, "Um . . . thank you? Are you being serious?"

Mom nodded. "Think of the live nativity our family puts

on every Christmas. You've been writing and directing that since you were three!"

Which is true. Remember the anxiety I had about the twins' birth and not being sure who should be baby Jesus?

Then Dad said, "And look at all those videos with your brothers that you put online. Maybe you can film your LARP Club and stick it up there too. Everyone loves watching the stuff you come up with."

I would be embarrassed to put my name on the patchy plotline our group came up with last week, but it's not a bad idea.

Also, they didn't say LARPing was dorky or anything, and listened and laughed when I explained that between volunteering at the shelter and my LARP character, I may develop a cat allergy.

I like my dad's laugh. And my mom's attention.

There, I said it.

But back to today. Fourth period. Super bizarre events occurred. In math class, Joel Lamier stopped at my desk during group time and said, "Hey, do you need your pencil sharpened?"

"I'm using a mechanical pencil."

"If you ever do, I'm a really good sharpener. I get the point super pointy."

"Thanks, but I'm . . . pointy enough."

And then Joel looked nervous talking to me. Actually nervous. I wondered if he had to go to the bathroom and had already used up his two free passes this year because he just kept standing there. "So . . . your brother is Luke Jorgensen, right?"

I wanted to say, "Yeah, that's why we have the same last name." But I controlled myself. Joel's pencils might be sharp, but he isn't. It didn't seem fair to throw him sarcasm. Maybe he can play Cornelious McDougerson, a very rich but rather daft gentleman who never quite understands a joke. Or he could wear a cardigan and fluff his hair and be a rugby player who got hit in the head one too many times.

"Cool," Joel said. "I just joined his volleyball club, High Impact? He's really good. Like hits the ball straight down every time."

"Yeah, I guess." It is so weird having people know you because of your siblings. You probably don't get it because Jason is so much older. But here I have pretty Talin and athlete Luke, and who am I? Oh, yeah. I have a pretend cat allergy.

"No, he's amazing."

"He played varsity as a freshman, and he said that's a big deal," I said. "Although he always thinks he's a big deal."

Joel laughed. I was being serious, not funny. Maybe I will put him in our party audience and he can do all that fake laughter they have on sitcoms. "Hey, Ryan. Come over here. This is Luke Jorgensen's sister."

Then Ryan came over, and they started asking me all these questions about Luke. And then Brittan Tanner came over because she's "going out" with Ryan.

"Are they boring you with sports?" she asked.

"No . . . just asking about my brother."

"Oh, I hate talking about my brother."

"Me, too," I mumbled. Although I love talking about the twins. And this was the first time that being related to Luke seemed like a good thing.

Then she laughed. It was like a regular comedy club. Mrs. Dudley had slipped out to the bathroom, otherwise we wouldn't have had that kind of freedom to yak it up.

"I like your scarf," Brittan said.

"Thanks. I knitted it."

"Shut up! You can knit? That is so cool."

And then I smiled. I can't remember the last time I had that much attention. It was almost overwhelming. Good overwhelming, like we were on the same page, not Bethany-Livingston-exclamation-point overwhelming.

"So do you think Luke would ever come play with us?" Joel asked. "We have sand courts in the neighborhood."

"I could ask him."

Then Mrs. Dudley walked in and told everyone to quiet down and go back to their seats. Ryan scribbled his number on a scrap of paper. "Text me if he's down. Thanks, Piper. That's cool of you."

Olivia, I have never talked to Ryan or Brittan. Joel is nice to me, but Joel is nice to everyone. The conversation was so weird, just one person after another joining in, and they all had nice things to say. And it felt . . . normal. Unusual, but normal at the same time. Like I really could invite them to my birthday party and I actually think they would come and be excited. And even if they didn't want to play certain characters and were just, like, regular people that . . . might be cool. Although I might need to force Luke to be there too. I'm not sure how this works.

Then, after school, I was hanging in the hallway, waiting for French Club to start. I could smell food in the room . . . bread, so I was totally right about the baguettes thing. Related: do they have an Italian Club at our school? Because:

I was just standing there when I saw blogger Bethany. I almost ran in before she saw me, but then she called my name.

"Hey, Piper!"

Too late. I turned around slowly.

"Hey! Tessa told me that you hooked her up with Danny. He's so cute."

"I guess."

"I would never even have the guts to talk to a boy."

"Uh . . . sure." I just kind of stood there, waiting for her to get to the point. In my experience, that's how a conversation goes. You do small talk for a second, then get to a topic— either asking something or sharing something. But Bethany didn't really do that.

"Are you going to Drama Club?" she asked.

"No, French Club."

"Oh, you should totally join Drama Club, P!" She actually shortened my name to one letter. "We have so much fun in there, and you'd be so good at it."

"How do you know?" I asked before I could stop myself. But seriously, how does she know what I'm good at?

"Because you're so good at speaking up in church class. I get so scared when the teacher asks questions, and you just pipe right in with the right answer all the time. Hey, get it? *Pipe?*"

I don't think she was making fun of me, but I couldn't tell for sure. "That's funny."

She laughed. "Anyway, come sometime. I'll see you at Souper Saturday next week, right? My mom is making my favorite tortilla soup."

"Yeah, I'm bringing my friend, Olivia."

"Perfect! 'K, bye."

I don't even know what happened. It's like I was wearing some people-attracting perfume. Which was in an episode of *Love and Deception*. Or have you ever heard the expression "jumped the shark"? (Sorry to bring up sharks.) It's when a show just kind of spins out of control. That's what today felt like.

I'm trying to figure out the character motives. Those boys talked to me because they worship my brother. And Brittan worships Ryan. And Bethany . . . I'm still not sure if I'm her church project. But . . . it was kind of nice. I really think Bethany would come to my party too. I'm almost halfway to filling up the guest list, and that's with taking off pretend ones like Trigger and the CVS cashier.

And, I don't know. Talking to people? About, like . . . random things. I don't totally hate it.

But don't tell anyone I said that.

I went to French Club after. I'll tell you all about it this weekend. I have extra math homework to do because I didn't get my problems done in class.

And my mom said you can come over for another late-over. (I keep telling her she can just call it "Olivia coming over." She doesn't have to keep calling it a late-over just because you never stayed all night when we attempted "sleepovers" at our house.) We can discuss what you'll wear at LEGO Club on Monday. Mom will even get us treats as long as we watch the twins while she runs to the grocery store. So text me a list of some fancy food you like, unless you want Goldfish crackers and applesauce. And don't even think we're going to order spinach pesto pizza again. Pepperoni. It's the American thing to do.

Night!

Piper

Grateful: that my brother finally did something useful for me (even if he doesn't know it), baguettes (they were warm!), pencil sharpeners, my mom really explaining my project in English so I can understand (even though she's busy and the birthday party is already the nicest thing any parent has ever done EVER), and HAVING YOU BACK ON MONDAY OR ELSE

Piper,

Look at me . . . back at school!

It was a little strange to be away for two days—kinda like when the TV announcer says "we now return you to your program, already in progress." It feels like I've missed a bunch of the plot and can't keep up. But I'm happy to be back and spending a quality fifty-two minutes each day with you in French class.

You're right . . . the rule should be one-day absences only. Even if you're coughing up an internal organ, GO TO SCHOOL. Deal?

Honestly, reading about how it went for you Friday at school—where you were wearing people-attracting perfume—was, how do I put this . . . hard to read. I mean, it makes perfect sense for people to want to talk to you. You have such a funny personality. An awesome smile. The world's cutest boots.

It just made me think . . . why does talking to people have to be so hard for me? All this planning and preparation—is something wrong with me? Am I missing the section of my brain that handles people skills? Or maybe I'm low on some essential vitamin . . . ? I keep forgetting to take my daily pill. (It's not a pill, of course. I'm still taking those Gummy Bear vitamins. Only the orange or green ones.)

I'm orange! I'm green! I'm yellow and get no respect.

I'm guessing that whole Savannah Swanson incident from third grade still haunts me.

But I'm in sixth grade now—I should have this figured out! Honestly, I just wish there was a formula I could follow.

I say that because of what happened today . . .

I took your advice to heart. Really, I did. The thing with the sharks and the unicorns? I gave it a shot. And it may have ruined my life.

But I'm guessing you've already heard.

Today in the cafeteria, I searched for an empty seat. I had to because I'd already stopped by Ms. Benson's and she was out sick today. Her office door was locked with this note tacked to it.

"Out sick the rest of the week. No counseling. And no organizing my office during lunch, Olivia."

She probably knew I'd try to get in there. Locked door, darn it.

So that's how I ended up in the cafeteria searching for a seat. The room had filled up quickly and open seats were a rare commodity. (On a side note: I'm not confident that the school staff has counted out the number of students versus the number of seats available. It's like an apocalyptic version of musical chairs. With lunch bags and trays.)

My heart sped up and I felt frantic. Where could I sit?

I recognized a couple of faces from our fifth grade class last year. Tara and her best friend, Jamie, who's obsessed with flavored lip gloss. There was one seat open on the end by them, but I wasn't sure if they were saving it for someone. You know what that meant: I had to ask the question.

"Umm, can I sit with you?" I barely squeaked it out.

Tara looked up at me as if I were some annoying door-to-door salesperson. But she didn't say anything—not a word. She just went back to chatting with Jamie. Was she being rude? Hard to tell.

So I sat down anyway, slowly easing into my chair like it was covered in thorns. Or maybe broken glass. It was an uncomfortable situation is what I'm saying.

Without hesitation, I whipped out my lunch and laid out a bag of Frito chips and some M&M's. Surely these would be my key to breaking into a new group of friends. Let the lunchtime bartering begin!

But when they pulled out their lunches, my jaw dropped through the floor:

French *macarons*.

Raw almonds.

Seaweed chips.

They had listened to Bethany's blog advice. Apparently junk food was now the uncoolest lunch item possible!

I quickly stuffed them in my backpack, but I'm sure Bethany is already blogging about my lunch fail. Defend me in the comments section, okay?

So there I was . . . trying to get Tara or Jamie or someone to acknowledge my existence. You would think I would've given up and run out of the cafeteria to save my reputation.

You.

Would.

Think.

But, no. That "Everything Is Awesome!" poster from Ms. Benson's office kept nagging at me and I knew I had to try to look on the bright side. Which meant I couldn't give up.

I took a deep, cleansing breath and said to Jamie, "I got

some bubblegum lip gloss this weekend. How about you?"

Nothing. No response. No one even looked my way. I could feel my heart beat faster and faster. It was up to techno-dance beat. Ohmygosh, ohmygosh . . . what was I supposed to do? Why were they ignoring me? I refused to hide out in the bathroom!

And that's when your advice came to mind. You know how you said that at lunch I could read interesting factual books about things like sharks or unicorns and become an expert on those things and then find other people who liked those things?

You said it's how I could make friends.

Well, I haven't started reading at lunch, but I have watched a bunch of reruns of Shark Week to get prepared. I'm not a shark expert yet, but I know a lot of shark facts.

So that's why without warning, I let out a sentence involving sharks.

A sentence I will regret until I'm a senior citizen.

"They're re-airing episodes from Shark Week. Anyone watch last night's *Man-Eater* show?" I asked it all loud and perky, counselor style. Then I horrifyingly added, "There was some very interesting information about the shark's mating behaviors, amirite?"

Tara looked over and crossed her arms. "We aren't talking about sharks. We're talking about something else."

With one head flip and swing of her hair, she shut me out. None of them would even look at me.

It was the Savannah Swanson incident all over again. I know you say I shouldn't bring that up anymore, but all those feelings . . . the humiliation, the embarrassment, the Immediate Stomachache . . . they all came back.

I realized I couldn't do this anymore.

I bolted out of the cafeteria and discovered that the fourth bathroom stall really isn't all that bad. Sort of roomy, actually.

But I can't live like this. Ms. Benson could get sick anytime, so I can't rely on the comfort of her office. I have to find a way to deal. And apparently sharing my new knowledge of sharks is not the answer. I have no doubt that if I'd tried to start a unicorn conversation, it would've ended in the same result.

Oh wait.
Unicorns are way
cute. Darn it!

Which brings me to this:

I know it's always been me and you . . . The Fearsome

Twosome. But I have to find a way to make more friends—people who talk to me, eat lunch with me, ask me questions.

Today made me realize that my problem isn't just trying to talk to Jackson . . . it's trying to talk to *anyone*.

So maybe I need to open up more—make some actual friends. I'm not exactly sure how I'm going to do that, but I'm going to try. Trying feels good.

I know it won't come between us. It just WON'T.

So. Deep breath . . .

LEGO Club is this afternoon. Am I ready to charmingly chat up Jackson? No. No, I am not.

I know we figured that all those practice clubs would give me time to rehearse my Chatting-People-Up skills. But worksheets and toe sprains and girls with tooth extractions got in the way, and the only real conversation I had was with that CVS cashier. So I'm going back to my original plan. . . .

Note passing. It's been done that way for centuries, and it was the primary form of communication during the Renaissance period. That's Shakespeare . . . *Romeo and Juliet*, all that. It's more romantic, don't you think?

So I went through our notes on that letter to Jackson and made a revised-revised-revised version. And it's not really so much "revised" as "brand-new."

J~

Let me know if you ever need help with math class. I totally know my positive and negative integers. It's kind of my thing.

And I had NO IDEA you were in LEGO Club, too! Hope you liked what I made. I'm thinking of adding a new wing to the house. Wanna help? You could come over tonight!

I like you. (heart drawing)
(a cute one, not a textbook one)

Olivia

So bold, right?! I think I'll give it to him just before the club ends. That way he can think about it overnight. No sense in pressuring him to answer me right then and there. Hopefully he'll tell me if he likes me too, and I can always play it cool if he doesn't like me, like "Oh, I didn't mean I LIKE like you." So there is still an out. And the *J* is the right mix of casual and friendly, don't you think?

You know what? Forget about me saying I'm not ready for this. I have a feeling that today is going to be the day that everything changes, Piper! I'll make new friends at LEGO

Club . . . you'll find all the guests you need for your party . . . Jackson will admit he likes me more than a friend . . . I'll create a LEGO house that blows everyone's mind. . . .

Sigh. (The happy kind.)

I take back all my worries above. Because right now, at this moment? I am loving my life.

I'll meet you this afternoon outside the door for LEGO Club. I'll have my note to Jackson in hand.

This is it, Piper. LET'S DO THIS.

Hopefully yours,

Olivia

Grateful:

1. Cool-looking bruises

2. Gummy Bear vitamins (the red ones are good too, actually)

3. You—dear Piper—for being the one to walk into that club with me today and give me all the confidence I need

4. My neighbor (that boy with an unusually high number of missing teeth) who let me borrow his LEGOs last night for practice

5. Our heart-shaped rock at our sacred tide pool spot

P.S. Just remember . . . me making new friends doesn't mean they will come between us. We're best friends forever. And that means FOREVER. We will sit on the same bench and feed seagulls when we are ninety-two. Cool?

P.P.S. Jackson Whittaker . . . here we come.

★ BETHANY'S BUSINESS ❤

HOME   NEWS   EVENTS   ABOUT   CONTACT

Bethanites!

It's been an amazing week, right? Before I get to
the good stuff, please keep me in your thoughts.
I've lost my favorite paisley-print headband. It was
last seen on the soccer field so PLEASE keep your
eyes out for it.

And now, moving on to my weekly installment...

THE RUMOR-MILL ROUNDUP!

★ I heard Mr. Marsdale—the math teacher—is now
the proud owner of a Labrador puppy named
Bones. Weird name, but keep complimenting
him on those puppy pictures so he stays in a
good mood.

★ SOMEONE apparently wrote a poem on the boys'

bathroom wall making an attempt at rhyme. Nothing rhymes with SKATEBOARD, guys.

★ I heard that NO ONE has joined the Yo-Yo Club and they're going to replace it with a Minecraft gaming club. Have fun, Creepers!

★ Speaking of clubs, there's one last rumor running around out there that I just HAVE to share. Emmy Carter heard from her cousin who heard from her neighbor that there was this guy in LEGO Club who said there was a HUGE fight that broke out today. Emmy was screaming all this to me over the phone—something about the nurse being called in and two girls were fighting—I don't know names—and then there was an explosion! Well, I'm not totally sure about that last part because my phone died and I had to fill in the blanks. But if you heard ANYTHING about what happened in LEGO Club, leave a comment! This type of thing is Bethany's Business!

Peace out, peeps!
Bethany

5 COMMENTS

QueenJenny21: OMG, I heard there were some broken bones. Or maybe it was broken LEGOs? And then a bucket of paint spilled and the LEGOs went flying everywhere. I am totally joining this club.

DjTyler: Naw, y'all. You got it all wrong! This one chick was flirting with a dude and then another chick was all, "WHUT?" and then someone got a bloody nose. Just normal stuff. Calm down, peeps!

GigiBarstow: Bethany, can you give me a shout-out?! I followed you, please follow me. You are super cool and awesome.

MaggieZ: I wasn't there, but I was next door practicing for Spelling Bee Club and the crashing sound was so loud that I actually put an extra *h* in the word "rhythmically." TOTAL. DISASTER.

Bethanyblogs: I still need more details! I'm dying to find out who got hurt! (And WHY, of course.) Get out there and find some answers, Bethanites!

To: loveanddeceptionfan@gmail.com

From: westonfamily706@yahoo.com

Subject: OMG! Are you okay??

Piper,

I'm so worried about you! All I remember was a big scuffle, some squeals, LEGOs flying in the air, and then Ms. Benson having to put a wet cloth on your nosebleed before she escorted you to the nurse's office. Please tell me you're not dead.

If you're not, then that's great because I need you to fix my life—the one that just fell apart. I can't believe that I went into LEGO Club this afternoon, simply trying to make a few friends and get a note to Jackson . . . but then I end up accidentally getting Jordan Goldberg—that guy with the plaid shirt and thick-rimmed glasses—to fall in love with me.

My life is over.

But really . . . are you okay? Please don't be dead. I need you. But also, don't be dead because you are awesome.

—O

To: westonfamily706@yahoo.com
From: loveanddeceptionfan@gmail.com
Subject: RE: OMG! Are you okay??

Liv,

I am still alive, but only barely. I have never seen my parents get so red-faced before. They've never talked to me that long without stopping to get a sippy cup for the twins or run my older siblings to another activity. I finally had uninterrupted one-on-one time.

And it was awful.

DAD: I just don't know what you were thinking, Piper.

MOM: We were so excited that you suddenly had interest in new activities—

DAD: And then come to find out that your real interest was vandalism!

ME: Come on, I don't know of many vandals who go to an Extreme LEGO Club. Don't let the extreme part fool you, those guys are puny.

MOM: And then to drive down to the school to find you—

DAD: With a bloody nose! You still haven't explained where you got the bloody nose.

ME: It's honestly not what you think. I was trying to help someone, I was being NICE.

DAD: Who were you trying to help?

ME: Tessa! From church. Her and Danny were LEGO partners, and then they got in an argument. I think it had something to do with the pink horse stable Tessa chose for them to build. I had to make a Winnebago with this kid named Gus. What kind of name is Gus?

MOM: Piper.

ME: So Danny asks if they can build a knight's castle instead, and Tessa said she hates anything to do with battle because she's a pacifist. Whatever that means. They went on like that for a while. Not that I was eavesdropping, because I was super into my Winnebago. Makes me sad I had anything to do with them going out. I should have known, because Georgina Davenport is this psychic on *Love and Deception*, and she would say that it's a bad combo since Danny is a Capricorn, and I'm pretty sure Tessa is a Leo—

DAD: Sweetie. Focus. Is this because you're doing so many clubs? Is it too much too soon?

ME: What?! I was having fun until . . . the incident. All the clubs I've been doing are fun. Next week, in LARP we get to—

MOM: What's a LARP?

ME: I told you. The role-playing club! You and Dad thought I was perfect for it. It even made the family white board! How can you not remember? (How could they not remember??) And anyway, it's been good for me to get out and meet new people.

DAD: We are happy that you're meeting new people. But look what happened. Danny Moss's parents are really upset.

ME: That's because Danny is a big fat liar! You haven't even let me explain the nosebleed yet.

MOM: Then explain.

ME: Okay, so Danny and Tessa have their lovers' quarrel. Then I ask them if they have any of those long green pieces for our Winnebago. You know, to distract them. Then Danny says, "Look, Piper, no offense, but I'm trying to talk to my girlfriend."

Then Tessa said, "I'm not your girlfriend anymore."

Then she threw a LEGO.

"That's real mature to throw a LEGO," Danny said. Which I do agree with. LEGOs are painful weapons. So then Tessa started tearing apart their horse stable! It was bonkers. Then Danny tried to stop her and he knocked into me and I fell over. Then Tessa yelled, "Don't push my friend!" So I, uh . . . kind of knocked into him and he fell into my Winnebago and my partner Gus started throwing

LEGOs. Then EVERYONE was throwing LEGOs and I took a window right to the nose and . . . yeah. It was extreme. But not WAY extreme.

DAD (*sighs*): We're going to discuss punishment. For now, let's take a little break from the clubs.

ME: But I HAVE to do clubs. I've made, like, an oath!

MOM (*very quietly*): Piper, you should not have shoved Danny. There has to be a consequence—maybe we should cancel this birthday party. If this is what happens around a room of LEGOs, then what's going to happen with pottery and paint?

ME: No! NO. Please, please don't cancel the birthday. (I swear my soul jumped out of my body and curled up on the floor. That's how sad I must have looked, because Mom said . . .)

MOM: Well, maybe we'll do your party somewhere else then.

ME: But there has to be a party. I've already started writing out subplots! I'll babysit the twins for the rest of my life, I promise. This whole thing is just a misunderstanding. Why won't you guys just listen?

MOM: Piper, we are listening. Your dad and I need to talk. For now, go to your room.

ME (*very dramatic exit with lots of stomping and slamming*

doors because I just got INJURED and it wasn't my FAULT and my parents never have time to LISTEN to me and if they take away my birthday party now it will be the end of my LIFE.)

Liv, I'm so sorry today didn't go how we wanted it to. Stupid Tessa and stupid Danny and their stupid breakup! I can't even think about my parents taking away my party. I would die. And who's going to want to come now? Who is going to like me enough to celebrate my birthday when Danny hates me like he does? Even if I hate him back.

Do I even need a soap opera-y birthday after all the DRAMA of today anyway?

I won't worry about it. I can't fix it now. Deep breaths, that's what you always say to do, right? So . . . tell me what was up with Jordan Goldberg? I think you're right that he's in LEGO love with you. I saw the way he looked at you—just after you gave him that note. Wait . . . why were you giving *him* a note? Weren't you going to give a note to Jackson? I was pretty confused with the bloody nose so maybe I saw it all wrong.

My nose really hurts, so I'm going to go lie down. You were right. LEGOs are cursed.

UGH!

P

Grateful: absorbent tissues, that look on Danny's face, how far you got on that project with Jordan (what was that thing?), Tessa calling me her "friend" when she started fighting with Danny, and lollipops (No reason. I just like lollipops.)

To: loveanddeceptionfan@gmail.com

From: westonfamily706@yahoo.com

Subject: Breathe, breathe, breathe

Piper,

Your parents are thinking about canceling the party? And no more clubs?! Take a deep breath. And another one.

Use your calm, hypnotizing skills to change their mind. You can do this. You HAVE to—it'll be the party of the year!

Now. Let me just say this . . .

Jordan Goldberg is a name that I do not want to ever hear again. Yes, there was a note-passing incident that occurred. And no, it wasn't to Jackson as planned. This is what you would define as "a tragedy."

Here are the bullet points of my now-tragic life.

- I was fully prepared to work on my two-story house alongside Jackson but Mr. Osaka put me over with Jordan Goldberg, despite all my throat-clearing and head-jerking motions toward Jackson, making it

OBVIOUSLY clear that Jackson was my future husband and this would be a pivotal point in our relationship, but NOOOO, I had to sit across from Jordan who was already mid-project.

- That project was not my choice.

- That project was . . . the Death Star.

- THE DEATH STAR, Piper.

- It's the most complicated LEGO project one can undertake; no cute little square house with adorable windows.

- I couldn't even figure out how to hold one of the spaceships right-side up so I got flustered and next thing you know my fist ended up smashing through the panel he'd just finished and HE SCREAMED LIKE HIS HOUSE WAS ON FIRE.

- This explains why absolutely no one else around us would talk to me or even give me eye contact and all I could do was hope and pray that Jackson hadn't heard all our commotion.

- Apparently he didn't hear it because he was too busy working on his farm scene with Dana Huffington.

- I am not a fan of Dana Huffington.

- But you knew this.

- She does that thing where she laughs and then punctuates it with a double-snort, like she's a cartoon character.

- But back to my tragic life . . .

- I figured that I had to make my move and give Jackson the note.

- So when I saw Dana go get a drink of water, I got up, the note stashed in my front pocket, and approached Jackson.

- When I was in front of him, I smiled, crinkled my nose all cute-like, then reached for the note in my pocket.

- But it wasn't in there. It was gone. The note had fallen out next to the Death Star! And guess where it was? In Jordan Goldberg's hands.

- He was reading it and smiling and his face looked flushed and OHNONONO he thinks I wrote the letter for HIM!!!

- It hit me that I never actually wrote Jackson's name on it. I wrote *J* to be all cool and casual. And, as you might have noticed, Jordan's name ALSO starts with *J*. Why couldn't I have had a crush on an Xavier?

- All of a sudden he wouldn't stop talking to me and

shrugging and stuffing his hands in his pockets and then kicking at rocks when he walked me out of the building and then smiling from ear to ear as he opened the car door for me.

- IT WAS A DISASTER.

I don't want to say it, but I have to. I think our lives are over. You got a bloody nose and your birthday might go back to frosted-fruitcake oblivion. I managed to get the wrong boy to fall in love with me and didn't find a single friend.

I'm starting to wonder if we'll ever be normal. It could be that it's just me and you and our dogs at the shelter. Maybe Blinkie and the twins when they are in the mood. You can knit and I can play chess. And that's the best we can hope for in life.

Your move, nerd.

That's not all that bad, is it?

Don't answer that. It's bad, I know. I promise Trigger will not be the only guest at your party (other than me, but a BFF doesn't really count as a guest, right? I'm like family—family who listens).

Well, I hope not.
Olivia

Grateful (really? How can I be grateful at a time like this?? But I guess that's the point.):

1. I'm grateful that I didn't get a bloody nose too because I don't think I can take one more After-School Club injury
2. The color blue
3. The color green (am I done yet? Two more . . .)
4. The color turquoise (yes, that's just blue and green)
5. And every letter besides the letter *J*

Olivia,

Let me start off with goodish news so I can pull you from the depths of despair.

I can still do some clubs! All is not lost! My mom was going through all my graded schoolwork and found the sheet from spelling club shoved in there.

"You went to Spelling Club?" She might as well have asked if I flew to Mars, that's how shocked her voice sounded.

"Of course."

"Wow, you're so talented with other things, honey. Like your movies and how you treat others. I didn't know spelling was your thing, though."

I shrugged. It kind of stung that my mom said that. I don't know why. "It's not. Birthday parties are."

Mom set down my folder. "Your dad and I talked. We think we might have overreacted a little."

You'll be so proud, Liv. I didn't roll my eyes or snort. "Yeah?"

"We talked to Danny's parents again. It seems like it was a

bit of a misunderstanding. Danny insisted it wasn't your fault at all."

Right? Danny-rhymes-with-fanny defended me? Seriously? I mean, it wasn't my fault. Clearly. But I was surprised that he would say anything positive. "So . . . I'm good? I can do clubs too?"

"Well, there still needs to be some sort of punishment. . . ."

"Clubs teach me new things," I said. "I'm all about learning."

Maybe I went too far with the "all about" part, but Mom's face got a little flushed, and she started humming. I think she's excited that I'm choosing to sPEll for fUn. Although I hope she doesn't think that I'm going to be good at spelling now.

I wonder if she ever thinks about that anyway? Like if she worries about me not being in all this stuff like Talin or Luke, or is she relieved that I'm not in activities because I would be one more stop on her chauffeur list, and also she would lose me as a babysitter?

Anyway, the agreement is that educational clubs are okay. And the birthday party is O-N. I would say thank you to Danny if I was, you know, talking to him.

Should I talk to him, by the way? I passed him in the hallway today and it was weird. Not the usual kind of weird we had before where he said something rude. This time he

WASN'T rude. I think I miss rude. I understood rude. Yes, he shoved me in LEGO Club, but I think it was an accident and I shoved him back. And he just broke up with his girlfriend and had a bruise on his arm bigger than Da Bruise.

I don't have time to write much because I am sitting by a lot of people and everyone wants to hear the story about Danny and Tessa's breakup. I really want to get this in your locker before class. That was so smart to give each other our combinations so we don't have to keep doing handoffs. And yes, it is fate that your combination is Jackson's birthday. Reversed.

This is who I'm sitting by:

1. Bethany

2. Tessa. Are you okay with me talking to them after the Savannah Swanson Incident? If not, I will stop. Promise.

3. Dana Huffington. I know. She asked to sit by me and I didn't know what to say.

4. Some guy named Brad who is eating hummus chips and if Jordan and Jackson don't work out, he might be your soulmate. Or maybe everyone is eating hummus chips now. Hey, what IS on your lunch menu now? Did you go back to your favorite foods or are you still Frito-ing it up?

5.   Troy Addelson. I've never talked to him in my life. I
      think he likes Bethany.

OK, more in a bit.

I didn't drop this off in your locker so I can finish this
note. Good thing, because we have a sub and she just passed
out these medieval-caste-system crossword puzzles.

Someone asked if they're graded and she said, "I think I'm
supposed to tell you yes, but they aren't really." So now we are
all just goofing off and I hope this lady doesn't lose her job.
Also, I hope she appreciates the effort I put into the bubble
letters.

I have to tell you what happened at lunch. Everyone agreed
that I was being a good friend when I stepped in on Tessa and
Danny's fight.

Tessa said it was unexpected, because Danny has always been so nice to her and he was the perfect boyfriend until that day. I asked her why they even started fighting, and she said Danny told her that the Moving Voices isn't really a good boy band, and I guess Tessa is a huge Moving Voices fan. It seemed like a stupid reason to me to get so mad (especially since they do stink), but I didn't say anything because everyone was talking to me and so excited.

I also wanted to say something about Danny getting me out of trouble with my parents, and the whole Not-Being-Mean-in-the-Hallway thing, but it seemed weird saying that with Tessa around.

So then I also mentioned that my birthday is next month and I *might* have a party, and they started talking like they were all invited already, and like they would actually come. I don't even think I could CAST all of them. It wouldn't be one soap opera episode—I could write a whole season! I need to update my casting sheet. I'm wondering if maybe I want to pull back on the drama a little now. Just to make the party a little, like . . . fun. For the guests. Or actors. Or whatever they're called.

Okay, this poor sub looks like she's going to cry. I'm going to fill out the crossword puzzle just in case.

Also, I had two thoughts.

1. What if I invite Jackson (NOT JORDAN) to my birthday party? Because apparently it's going to be a guy/girl party now. Not guy/girl like we are going to do stupid kissing games, just there will be both guys and girls. And you're a good artist so you can impress him with your skills painting pottery! What a great SCENE that would make. Would it be too over the top to have music playing in the background while you two talk?

2. I really thought hard about clubs, and although I wouldn't mind watching you "play" badminton again, I think the next one we should do, and really commit to, is Chess Club. It's educational, so my mom will keep thinking I'm a well-rounded child who enjoys doing all sorts of activities. And you love chess. I know you said thinking about playing with someone besides your dad gave you achy insides, but you also said you think your dad wants you to beat him in a game. Chess Club would up your skills so you could.

Also, I know I said I thought chess was boring. But that time I got so bored when you tried to teach me was years ago.

I've matured. I'm sure I'll like it since you and I are so alike.

So far, the clubs have been surprisingly fun. Especially LARP. But that's not why we started, right? This is about helping you talk to people. It's about me finding actors! Maybe even actors who could be friends, because I kind of feel like that's what some of these people are turning into. Not that YOU aren't still my best, best friend. The Jackson/Olivia and Piper/Soap Opera Star (I still haven't decided which soap star will be the lucky groom) double wedding is totally going to happen, with red flowers or blue flowers or whatever you want. By the way, can Blinkie be our ring bearer?

3. Oh, and that Souper Saturday is the Saturday before Thanksgiving, only two weeks away. I know it's far, but make sure your mom can drop you off since Luke has a tournament and my mom can't pick you up.

That's it!

Piper (who has developed a love for exclamation points apparently. Sorry about that)

Grateful: See that list above? I MIGHT HAVE AN INVITE LIST

Piper,

You're right—I should go to a club where I can learn something, a skill. Just educational clubs from now on.

Let's do this, Chess Club. It's possible it'll be even better than watching that British guy on YouTube who teaches chess, and I'll finally figure out a way to beat my dad. And surprise him. Impress him, maybe.

I'd like that.

Okay, social-status-update alert: today after third period I was getting a sip of water over in the math wing, and a bunch of kids were crowded around Troy Addelson's locker. There were so many of them and I couldn't tell who was talking, but the conversation basically went something like this:

—Do we have math next?
—Yes. Oh, did you guys hear about that Piper girl having some huge birthday party?
—Ohmygosh, yes! I totally want to go.
—Yeah, totally!

—Do we need to take our math book to class?

—Troy, yes!

—And that Piper girl seems pretty cool. How did we not know her before?

—I want to get invited. How do I get invited?

—And a pencil?

—TROY!!!

—Find a way to get me invited to that party—I have to go!

Piper, seriously. That mob of kids talked about you almost the entire time if you subtract the moments where Troy Addelson had no idea how to be prepared for class. It was like when your dad was in that Mr. Brake commercial. But bigger.

This is amazing, right? It doesn't surprise me, really. You definitely have this people-attractant thing about you, and it has nothing to do with perfume. It's just YOU. And I know that you've always said in the past that you were happy with it just being me and you. Two peas, one pod—all that stuff.

But Piper . . . they were saying THE NICEST things about you. And maybe someday all your people skills will rub off on me, and someone (probably not a mob) will say nice things about me.

And I'm okay if it's the girls from your church class. At

least I think I am. Maybe I could *try* to be okay with it? Sometimes I'm not sure *what* to be okay with.

When we get to Chess Club, I'm going to stick by your side. I'm going to learn some new things hopefully. And I'm going to stop pressuring myself to find new friends and a husband for the double wedding and eternal happiness all in one afternoon. I'll get there eventually.

The fact that I'm saying all these things reminds me how lucky I am to have you for a best friend. You always manage to put all the right words together to make me look on the bright side of life.

I hope I can do the same for you.

Which is why I have come up with a great idea . . . it involves me, you, our notebook, and a short bus ride.

Meet me at the tide pool after school. And make sure to bring the notebook!

With good secret surprise excitement,

Olivia

Grateful for:

1. That I've gotten my locker combination right on the first try for the ENTIRE day (I remember the numbers but there are so many twists and turns required!)

2. Friendly mobs

3. Us joining Chess Club

4. Going to Souper Saturday with you (so! much! togetherness!)

5. And the piece of homemade cornbread that Mom stashed in my lunch

Here we are at the first annual "Blessing of This Awesome Notebook," where we will use this holy tide-pool water to bless this book. By the way, this is an awesome idea, Liv. What's a more sacred setting than the ocean? And the heart-shaped rock we found last summer is still here. It's a sign! We should've done it sooner.

Is it weird we're writing all of this down and not talking to each other?

Not weird. Genius. And it's what the notebook would want us to do. Think of the notebook, Liv.

Sorry. I will only consider the feelings of this not-alive object from now on.

Thank you. The ceremony has begun. All rise.

Rise?

You said I could be Master of Ceremonies. Hold on... let me get into character. [pause] Here ye! Here ye! Let it be known that on this day, we besmeech or

besmirk—oh, wait. I don't know the word.
Is it decide?

Maybe less British and more California-ish?

You always know how to make me smile. Hold on.
Gotta get into the character of ME. [pause] Piper &
Olivia agree to use this notebook to share our deepest
thoughts. Our hopes, our dreams.

And our secrets.

Oh, and notes to boys!

Of course. And let's agree that we—the Fearsome
Twosome—will always have this heart-shaped rock by
the tide pools for our sacred meeting place. Remind
me next time that we should only come right after
low tide. And we should probably keep in mind that
pelicans love to fly right over this spot and how they
love to aim their droppings at tourists. There's no
way they can tell we're locals—

All right, all right, Chatty Chatterson. Let's finish

the ceremony. Is it cool if I sprinkle the book with holy sand?

Very cool.

Hands in—this book is our protected sacred notebook. And I promise that we will always stay best friends. Even though we have agreed to expand our horizons and make new friends, it will NEVER come between us. I PROMISE.

No one will ever come between us. I PROMISE.

Meeting adjoined!

Adjourned.

Eeek! The pelicans are coming!

I tried to run.
I hate pelicans.

poop

KENNEDY MIDDLE SCHOOL CHESS CLUB

Don't miss out on our school tournament!

All winners will advance to the regional tournament and can win a gift certificate to Chevy's restaurant!

Piper,

I have three words for you: You. Were. Right.

That was such a blast. From the "Chess Is the Best" song they all sing at the beginning, to the stretches they use to warm up (my personal favorite was the one where we contorted our body to look like the knight), to the handshaking ritual before we sit down, to the GAME ITSELF, to my partner who was Ellie Thompson and I know we've never talked to her before because she does that thing where she won't ever look at you and always appears to be staring at a spot on the floor, but I found out that she is awesome, and holy cow that was all one sentence!

Ellie and I played and talked and played and talked and she told me about how she learned chess from her older brother. But he just moved off to college and now she feels weird about playing with anyone else and, Piper, IT'S LIKE WE'RE TWINS! She totally understood how I felt about only playing it with my dad. And we even talked about how our chess moves are like trying to get through life in middle school—always making one move at a time, but thinking three steps ahead so we don't get humiliated. We laughed and talked some more.

And then Ellie promised to come sit with me at lunch. Like the way friends do. She promised to help me get better at chess and who knows . . . maybe I'll win that gift certificate to Chevy's! Dad loves those nachos—there's no way he could resist.

A couple of times I leaned over to get your attention— give you a thumbs-up and stuff. But it looked like something was in your eye? You kept rubbing at it. And then one time I noticed you were just staring at the ceiling. I do that too when I'm trying to figure out my next chess move. Was Steve Polaski good? He's the captain; he must be. I hope he taught you a few things. If you have any problems with the rules, let me know. Chess is challenging, but not impossible. I mean, I learned when I was three. And I taught Blinkie. Sort of.

Wow. Today was so much fun, right? Who knew that I'd love it this much!

Well, you did actually. Because you are the smartest girl I know.

Your forever Chess Buddy,

Olīvīa

Grateful:

1. Chess tournaments
2. Gift certificates to Chevy's
3. Knight stretches
4. Meeting Ellie Thompson
5. And educational clubs!

Olivia,

Yeah. Chess club. I'm glad you liked it. I knew if you just did something that you loved, you'd feel comfortable and relax a little and be yourself. Because *yourself* is a good thing. Ellie seemed really nice and funny and that's so cool that you hit it off. Ms. Benson is going to be so lonely and unorganized now at lunch without you there to hang her motivational posters.

I am maybe a little confused how it all works. Like in checkers, you can only go on the red squares, so when you have pieces on ALL the squares, it seems crowded. And I had to keep counting the spots I could move with that horsey piece. I can go three over and two up, right? Something like that. I was really good with the regular pawns, because those ones you just move forward, but then Steve knocked those out in like two seconds. I'm sure he was doing that thing you said you do at school—planning his third move while he was doing his first move. I'm not sure my brain can do that. Why do you think this is fun again?

Ick. Steve Polaski. He was such a know-it-all. Every time

I tried to move a piece, he would suck in his breath like I was about to push a button to detonate a bomb.

"You can't move that there."

"Why not?"

"Because that's the rule."

"Well, sometimes when I play Monopoly with my family, we change the rules to make the game go faster."

Steve is oily and clears his throat too much like Randall Menard in *Love and Deception*. And you know how I feel about Randall.

Steve smirked. "I'm going to beat you in three moves. Don't worry about this going faster."

I slid the bishop diagonally, LIKE I'M SUPPOSED TO, and then he knocked it down with . . . seriously, what are those horsey things called again? "Steve, rules are for borings."

"Just because I'm good at chess doesn't make me boring. Don't stereotype."

Olivia, I don't want to sound stupid, but what does stereotype mean again? I would have asked Steve, but I think that would have made him more smug.

"I also play rugby, saxophone, and design video games," he said. "I'm very well-rounded."

"That's great, Steve. I . . . make videos. And babysit. And knit. And volunteer at the animal shelter. And I'm in Spelling

Club and LARP Club and . . . I'm thinking about badminton."
So that was a stretch. But he was bugging me.

"Cool. Maybe you should go to one of those clubs now."

"Why?" I asked.

"Checkmate."

"Excuse me?"

Steve rolled his eyes. "I just won, Piper. You know, there are some cookies in the back. If you want to go eat, I can stay here and play against myself."

That was probably the point where I got something in my eye. I'm pretty sure he was calling me stupid. Which hurt. He is probably one of those guys who would have laughed at me when I was having a hard time in reading class. Guess who is NOT going on my birthday invite list, even if he is the perfect guy to play Randall.

But it's cool. We aren't going to love everything an equal amount. Besides, it's only like once a week, right? I'll pick it up soon. I'm a Sagittarius and we don't quit.

At least not right away. And I'm not even sure about my zodiac knowledge because they killed off the psychic on *Love and Deception* last week anyway. Maybe I should start learning about life and the news from other sources, right?

But I am so so so happy that you met Ellie. I am so happy you are having fun. I want you to know that. When something good happens to your best friend, it's almost like it's happening to you. Or me. Gah, always mixing up when to say you and me.

Oh, and hey, I'm glad we can finally do LARP together this week! Did you want to just stick to the clubs we've already done or try any other new ones? Sea Club looks fun. Love me some new educational activities. (And friends!)

Piper

Grateful: Those cookies in the back, everyone wants to come to my party!!, you having fun, imagining myself sticking a pawn up Steve's nose, and the theory of relativity (because that's something that SMART people like me enjoy, even if I don't know what it means yet)

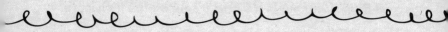

Piper,

Don't worry, I don't know much about the Theory of Relativity either other than it has something to do with the time-space continuum. And E=MC². And Einstein bringing his A-game.

Speaking of A-game, don't let Steve bother you. Sounds like he was pretty rude—what a chess snob. But at the next meeting we get to switch partners, so I'm sure it will go much better.

Just do yourself a teeny-tiny favor . . . try not to use the phrase "horsey piece." I personally think that you using it is understandable/adorable, but other people might, you know, go full Chess Snob on you. I'm guessing everyone in there would do that, actually. I mean, taking a look around that room I could tell they were all WAY into it, given all the nail biting and forehead wrinkling that was going on. I was surrounded by kids who constantly thought three moves ahead.

Which means one thing: I'VE FOUND MY PEOPLE.

Why did I think that I should only play with my dad? Now I'll learn how to get better AND help us find new friends. (Are you calling them friends now or still characters? I think you've crossed over. Make *friends*. I'm sure it will still be dramatic, whoever you invite.)

Counting Ellie, we only have a couple more to go. And that will be simple. At the next club we're playing doubles. That's two more people for me to get to know, and BAM, we've got ourselves a fully attended party!

I know, I know . . . exactly how do I know about us switching partners at the next meeting, you ask? OH! Let me tell you a little story . . . it's about me . . . in the lunchroom . . . not eating alone or desperately talking to strangers or bringing the wrong food item for exchange. This story is NONE of those things.

This story is about me, walking into the cafeteria today while feeling a loneliness stomachache about to come on, when suddenly I see two hands waving at me from the corner. It was Ellie, flailing both hands in the air. "Come sit with us!" she called out.

And that's when I noticed Ellie was surrounded by a group of girls. They were all girls from Chess Club, and one of them—get this—had a spiral notebook with a unicorn wearing nerd glasses on the cover. TOUCH. DOWN.

We all talked about the club and our history teacher and unicorns and even Shark Week. It was like I'd stepped into an alternate reality where people actually liked me—people who weren't you or my relatives. (Wait, maybe that's what Einstein was talking about with his theory of relativity? I'm guessing his middle school years were bumpy too.)

How do I say "Whassup, dude?" in physics?

So then Ellie gave me the heads-up on how we're playing doubles at the next club meeting. OH! Speaking of club meeting, it doesn't meet one day a week. Didn't you see the poster? It meets THREE days a week plus Saturdays. Apparently they meet so often because they're preparing for the regional tournament. They pick the four top players, and I really want to be one of those top four! We play against Monterey and Santa Barbara and Fresno schools, so it's a really big deal. I know it might be a stretch to think you'll make it to the tournament, but don't worry—you're just starting out. By next year, you may be caught up with me. (Again, no more saying "horsey piece." Okay? Love you, thanks.)

This all means we can't go to LARP, of course. Or French or Spelling Club. Our schedules are going to be full, my dear!

So this Saturday when we meet for Chess Club, I'll ask my mom to come pick you up and then—OH. WAIT.

This Saturday is that Souper Saturday thing at your church. It's not that important, right? Just let them know something came up. Did you really want to be friends with those girls? Even with the Savannah Swanson Incident, I'm fine with it, I guess. But maybe be friends with them later, after Chess Club, because you already have so many people lining up!

And after Chess Club, let's see if my mom will take us to the mall so we can do that thing where we people-watch and make up stories about the secrets people are hiding. I love that story you told about that woman wearing a long frumpy skirt. You told me she used to be the famous fashion designer Annabelle Dior, but her runway show got a nasty review in the *New York Times* and now she dresses like a shopping bag just to spite the critics. Seriously, I loved that one.

And then we'll go split a soft pretzel. With mustard, of course.

The girl who will soon have mustard on her chin,

Olīvīa

Grateful:

1. Einstein's middle school theories

2. Ellie's waving hands that were aimed right at me

3. Girls who like nerdy unicorns
4. My mother for agreeing to drive me to Chess Club and then take us to the mall (she hasn't agreed yet, so this is technically a PRE-grateful)
5. Annabelle Dior's dark secret past

Piper—

I'm at the shelter. In between
lessons with Trigger, I keep
peering out the window to look
for your mom's car.
 Where are you?

Olivia

Olivia,

Sorry I missed the shelter last night. I was busy. Did you go, or were you playing chess? And sorry I didn't call you back. I was still busy. And maybe not so much busy as a little annoyed.

You want to give up all the other clubs? Even LARP, which was super fun? And Spelling Club, which wasn't super fun, but people were at least nice? I'd even go to Extreme LEGO Club with Danny again if I had to.

Obviously, I don't love Chess Club. I don't think the people there are chess snobs. I think they are just snob snobs. Every other club I've been to, people tried to make me feel welcome. It wasn't just Steve who was mean to me. Everyone kept looking at me like, "Why are you here? You're too stupid."

And I know a horsey thing is a knight, okay? But why don't they just call it a HORSE instead of a knight? Maybe in the old days, that worked, but chess needs to get with the times.

So I'm not going back. I know I said Sagittarians don't

quit, but I decided if people are mean, quitting is a good thing. My parents said I could still go to clubs, and I will. All the other clubs we went to. Maybe new ones. I don't even know. I really need to focus on planning my birthday party anyway. More Chess Club would probably mean a bloody nose for Steve Polaski, and then the party would be completely kaput.

But you. You love it. And that is SO GREAT, really. Keep going. Keep eating lunch with your friends. I am honestly glad you found a little home. Just because we like different things doesn't mean we can't still be close. Sure, we won't have Souper Saturday (or the mall after Chess Club, since Souper Saturday is an all-day thing), but we can still do Mondays at the shelter and, of course, my Party of Epic.

Oh, and if you want to add Ellie to my invite list, that'll be great. Well, maybe. I really need to figure out the list now that everyone is talking about it. People keep coming up to me and asking me when the party is, like it's an open invitation. Our lunch table was totally packed today, and Jackson Whittaker even came over and sat there for a little.

I probably should have mentioned that first with a bunch of hearts and exclamation points, huh? Here you go, better late than never:

JACKSON WHITTAKER!

JACKSON: Hey, Piper.

ME (*trying to cover shock that Jackson knows my name*): Hey, Jackson.

JACKSON: So are you coming back to LEGO Club after your Danny fight?

ME: I don't know. I got sort of grounded after that, so I have to convince my parents I won't get violent and that LEGOs are educational.

JACKSON: They are. We build stuff.

ME: I know, I told them we're improving our spatial ability. We'll see if that works. (*I only knew the word "spatial" because I looked it up the night before to strengthen my argument with my parents so they'd let me go to LEGO Club again. They've been holding out on that one.*)

JACKSON: And . . . uh, what about your friend, Olivia? Jordan said she fell in love with him there.

ME: THAT DID NOT HAPPEN.

(Then I think Jackson got scared because he started to scoot away.)

JACKSON: Okay. Well, cool. I will . . . let Jordan know. He'll be bummed. He thinks Olivia is cool. I mean . . . she *is* cool.

ME *(switching from mean-sounding to so so so excited)*: She is! The coolest! The best! You should talk to her sometime! I mean, not that she's sitting around waiting for you to. But you should!!!

(I know. I failed you a little. It was all that screaming in your letters bursting out of me.)

JACKSON *(smiled!)*: All right. I hope you both come back to LEGO Club. See ya.

END SCENE

I know I'm the one who knows nothing about boys or dating clues. But that sort of seems like interest to me, Olivia.

So it might be the perfect window to invite him to my party? I didn't know he was friends with Jordan. Maybe I should invite both of them so it's not too obvious? Even though my invite list is about to explode to twenty and my mom might need to sell one of the twins to pay for all the extra pottery.

I need to get SERIOUS about this party already. Only a

couple weeks to go. I really think I need to ditch the casting and just invite people. For time reasons.

Sorry I'm quitting Chess Club. I know you understand.

Piper

Grateful: Never having to see snobby Steve Polaski again, knowing I'm NOT STUPID just because I have reading comprehension issues and don't totally understand chess, having so many people to sit next to at lunch, LARP, and my mom cooking tacos tonight

Hi, Mrs. Jorgensen. It's Olivia. I emailed Piper but she didn't answer. I called but it was busy.

Sorry, sweetie. Everything okay?

Yes. Sure. I mean, relatively. It's a complicated question.

Sounds like you need to talk. Hold on, I'll hand the phone to Piper.

Hey

Hey

Sooooo . . .

I read what you wrote.

Okay. Are you . . . mad?

Me? No. Great. Super fine. I'm actually thinking about how you talked to Jackson. And he said I was cool?

Yep. So awesome, right?!

Yep.

Olivia.

What?

What's wrong? I can tell there's something wrong. Do you want me to call you?

It's okay.

You're acting weird.

No I'm not. In fact, I think we should get going on our plans for our double wedding.

Pink-and-purple theme, right?

You know me better than that. You can have pink or purple. Not both. How about pink and orange?

Gross.

Aqua?

Maybe. And I'm thinking of switching from peonies to orchids. They were used in ancient Greece and were a symbol of love and beauty. You know how much I want to have a Greek wedding.

But I liked peonies. I looked them up. They make the bouquet look bigger. How do you make a bouquet out of long skinny flowers?

We already decided. You get to pick the people—caterer, musician, wedding planner. That way you can create whatever story you want with their lives. I'm flowers.

It's not a big deal. We can just do both.

We can't have *both*. We either stick with the theme or we don't. If I force myself to get behind a flower I'm not passionate about, then that's going to show in my bridal photos! You either support me in this or you don't, and I feel I should express my disappointment to you. I can only sacrifice so much.

Wow, did that take you forty-five minutes to type out or what? Why are we texting instead of talking?

Greek-themed weddings with orchids are what's best for ME. And maybe you shouldn't spend all your time worrying about the guest list. Why can't you just try something that I want to do simply because we're best friends? Don't go off and do peonies on your own.

We're not talking about our double wedding anymore, are we?

I want you to come to Chess Club. With me.

But that wasn't our plan. We wanted to try a bunch of clubs. You haven't even tried LARP yet. So you're going to give up everything else just for chess?

Of course I am. And you're the one who said we'd commit to Chess Club. Getting better at chess is a big deal for me!

Which means you think Souper Saturday isn't that big of a deal. I've been looking forward to it for weeks. I know I didn't say it, but . . . I don't know. I like having all these things to do and people to be with.

I just don't have time to go, that's all.

What kind of club meets FOUR DAYS A WEEK? That's not a club. That's a full-time job.

It doesn't feel like a job. I'm really liking it.

I . . . I just wish you were going to Souper Saturday with me. I feel like you're ditching me a little bit.

I'm sorry.

Gotta go. Finn just dragged the dog into the bathtub. Mom needs my help.

You don't have a dog.

I know!

Text me later?

Piper?

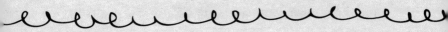

Piper,

I'm not really sure what to say . . . or how to say it. I guess I figured you'd want to do Chess Club because that was our agreement—find a club we both like and go together so we can find friends. Or I could learn to have conversations and you could play casting director. Whatever the reason, we started this together.

Together . . . like always. Me. And you.

I had no idea you were feeling so "stupid," as you say. Because you're NOT. You're Piper, and everyone adores you as soon as they get to know you.

The only reason why you don't have a lot of friends is because you CHOOSE not to. Whether you realize it or not. Maybe it's because you're only comfortable hanging out with me . . . or maybe it's because you're incredibly loyal to me . . . or maybe you just don't like too many people being around you because you live in the middle of a litter of kids, I don't know. My guess is it's probably all of that.

But it's all different for me. At my house, now that Jason is gone, it's just me. You say that you feel just as ignored at home as I do, but I don't see how that's possible. You have to escape to the bathroom just to talk on the phone. Me? I have only my cat to worry about. Sometimes Blinkie takes time out from her kitty naps to glare at me, but other than that I don't have much "social interaction" at home.

And when I said you're VERY loyal to me . . . as much as I don't want to admit it . . . sometimes I think that's exactly why you spend all your time with me. Yes, it goes back to that Savannah Swanson Incident in third grade. Yes, you tell me all the time to block that out of my memory and never mention it again. Yes, you're usually right.

I said I'd try to be okay with you being friends with those girls from church who were in Savannah's group, but I can't get that day out of my head, Piper. It feels like it would take brain surgery.

That memory haunts me.

It wasn't so much that I showed up for Savannah's end-of-the-year school party and no one was there. It wasn't even that she and all her crew laughed at me the next day when they said it had been canceled and they forgot to tell me. And it wasn't even the fact that I overheard them in the bathroom saying that they intentionally told me to go to a different place because they think I'm such a NERD.

It was the part where I had to explain it all to my dad. He kept hounding me about what happened, and he even called the teacher to find out why it was canceled. You have no idea how embarrassing it is to have your teacher call and explain why you were left out of a party. Or how humiliating it is when that teacher calls in the world's most popular girl, Savannah Swanson, and gives her detention. Or how awful it is that none of those girls from third grade will even look my way anymore, including your church friends Eve and Tessa.

I was scared to even talk to *anyone* after that whole ordeal.

That potted pink chrysanthemum you dropped off at my house after the whole Savannah thing went down was the sweetest. I loved it. And I'm glad you gave me a fake one because it won't ever die. I keep it on my nightstand to remind me of you . . . that Piper Jorgensen is always on my side.

And I know you say I shouldn't bring up the incident. But there are reasons why making friends is so hard for me. So once I walked into that Chess Club, and felt comfortable— for the first time in years—I started to think maybe I could finally shake off that whole humiliating incident.

So it's okay if you don't want to go to Chess with me. It's

probably time I step out on my own and start to make friends by myself. Fly away, baby bird!

Flapping my wings,

Olivia

Grateful for:

1. Two days off of school
2. Chess Club again on Saturday
3. Mom letting me cook my vegan corn casserole
4. Never having to see Savannah Swanson again
5. My fake pink chrysanthemum
6. OH, AND JACKSON AT YOUR PARTY

Hey, Olivia,

So, Savannah Swanson. I guess we talk about it.

That was awful. SO awful. I can't imagine how bad you must have felt. It was really rude of Savannah, who moved to South Dakota anyway and GOOD RIDDANCE, to laugh at you and be mean in front of others like that. But I'm starting to wonder now if those girls feel bad about it too. I mean, Eve is nice. So is Tessa. They all are. Maybe they weren't really a part of Savannah's meanness. Maybe they just happened to be there. Maybe they felt awful about it too. Maybe, Liv.

Okay. Can we shake it off? Just for now?

I *have* to tell you about Souper Saturday—I had so much fun. It was pretty much the best day of my life. I don't think I've ever laughed that hard. Bethany Livingston is so funny when she's not acting all smart! We were supposed to tie blankets all day, but we kept tying other things into the blanket. And they had these candy-cane brownies that were just amazing. Tessa and Eve were there too. And we had this whole joke about monkeys, because Tessa brought this jungle-print fabric. A lady would come in to the church gym to work on a blanket and we would try to think of a way to talk about monkeys in the conversations:

"I bet this baby will be BANANAS for her blanket!"

"What flavor is this lollipop? APE?" (Instead of grape. Get it?)

By the end, we were just making gorilla noises and throwing bananas back and forth. Maybe you had to be there to get it. Hilarious.

We got SOOO many blankets done! The lady who organized all the activities was so excited, she wants to host a sewing night with the girls and have us make more stuff. Then I said I can knit and everyone thought that was the coolest thing ever. So we're going to start knitting things at Tessa's house on Thursdays. She wants us to set up a store in her neighborhood like Danny does and sell even more. Maybe we'll do an online shop someday. I mean, if they're any good at knitting. But I bet they will be. They're such awesome girls. I'm glad I gave them a chance despite You Know What.

And you really missed out on the soups. Even the organic kinds you like were yummy. I got the recipe for the enchilada one and I made it for my family last night using some leftover turkey from Thanksgiving. My brothers each ate two bowls and my mom was so relieved to not have to cook that she said she thinks clubs really are a good idea. Educational, non-educational, just as long as we're talking *school* clubs I can go to any of them.

Her one rule was I had to write an apology note to Danny and invite him to my party, but that's a small price to pay for all the fun we're going to have. I don't know what I'm going to come up with to say to him. I hope Tessa will understand that I have no choice about inviting him.

My sister told me Danny probably likes me and that I've been doing my hair cuter lately (have I?), which was really nice for her. First to speak to me at all, and then to say something positive. Although double gross on Danny. Like he even would.

I'm glad you feel like you're able to make friends now. Me too. I always thought having a lot of sort-of friends would be more work, but it really isn't. You just laugh in the group, say a couple of funny things, and it's all good. Oh, I invited all the church girls to my birthday! I really need to go over this list one more time before I write out invitations. My mom's going to do them with me tomorrow. I get to pick them out from her stationery shop. Just me and her. Cool, right?

But sorry, back to you. That's great about the regional tournament. Good luck at your first match tonight. I would totally come and watch, but I don't have a ride and I want to go to LEGO Club. They're building famous Washington monuments now. And I'd rather not run into Steve Polaski and his Eyes of Judgment.

I just hope Chess Club doesn't swallow up your whole life until you forget about all the other things that matter to you. But it probably won't. How much chess can a person really play anyway?

NOT EVERY DAY, RIGHT?!

Later skater!
PIPER

Grateful: Monkeys!, broccoli cheese soup, eating with my whole family, picking out paper for my invitations, seeing you again today, and everything is good again ☺

Piper,

You won't believe this. The Chess Club always meets after school but . . . guess what? Last night we held a special meeting and we all went to Dairy Queen! Twelve of us took over the back three booths, all with the manager's consent. (He also happens to be Ellie's dad so I think he was just happy to watch her play.)

We played two games with a partner, then rotated (but we got breaks so we could fill up on Oreo Blizzards). And then the two top players who won the most matches were given a gift certificate . . . to Chevy's!

So how did I do at my matches, you ask? I'm not gonna lie . . . I killed it! I went on the offensive more, didn't subordinate my pieces, protected the queen, and used my bishop for sneak attacks—all the things Dad taught me. And it worked! I played six games and won five, only losing to Steve Polaski, but part of me wonders if I didn't let him win. He IS the club captain, and when I took both his rooks, I could see sweat forming on his forehead. And then he started to develop an eye twitch. Poor guy.

I won five matches and now I have a Chevy's gift certificate! That means I can ask Dad to take me and hopefully we'll talk about . . . I don't know . . . STUFF!

I have no idea yet if I made it into the top four to move on to the regional tournament, so I'm crossing my fingers and toes (but not my elbows anymore because it hurt after a few minutes). They let us know this afternoon, so cross your elbows for me since you're flexible.

Okay, so it wasn't just winning five matches that made my night. Afterward, we all hung out outside on the patio and ate corn dogs and French fries. Then Ellie and I and a bunch of other people (I won't bore you with everyone's names because you don't know them) made French fry castles, just like you and I used to do with your Tater Tots, except that Ellie has this amazing ability to lay down crinkle fries like she's making a log cabin and the base of our structure was indestructible. We were able to go up three floors! And then, you won't believe it, the guys started breaking up pieces of their corn dogs into little miniature people and we made up this whole scene where Lord Corn Dog was being taken over by the evil Darth Blood (which was actually a blob of ketchup with dabs of mustard for eyes—sounds silly, but it really did look sinister).

It was like I glided among them gracefully like an Olympic skater. You should've been there. But you're busy with the soup stuff and it sounds like you changed your mind about those girls and had fun, so that's good. Right? That's a good thing?

I want to believe it's a good thing—I really do.

So today I was at lunch and Jordan grabbed some extra napkins for me when he noticed I didn't have any. I was sitting with Ellie and he laid them down next to me and said, "I had some extras—thought you might need some." And he shot me this I'm-such-a-nice-guy smile.

Yeah, Jordan may be a nice guy, but I never meant for him to read that note and suddenly start acting like Mr. Wonderful. I meant for Jackson to be my Mr. Wonderful. Even though I asked him in math class if he wanted me to sharpen his pencil since I was headed that way and he just shrugged and didn't say anything. I don't get it—maybe he had a Math Headache? I get those sometimes when I'm solving a word problem.

But honestly, I sort of feel like I don't have time to deal with either one of these guys. Chess is taking up my free time, and when I'm not doing homework, I'm studying chess tutorials on YouTube.

So last night my dad walked in on me. "Whatcha watching?"

I quickly clicked my tab over to a *Gilmore Girls* episode since I didn't want him to know that I was studying chess. My plan is to wait until I'm chosen for the regional tournament, then leave the tournament invitation on the kitchen table under his travel coffee mug and surprise him.

"I'm watching season two, episode five."

Dad nodded. "A wise choice."

"Wanna watch with me?" I patted my bed and scooted over to make room. It would also be the perfect time to spring the Chevy's gift certificate on him.

"Can't tonight, gotta grade papers."

"How about we play a game real quick?" I asked, gesturing toward the chessboard.

He looked at the carpet, not me. "Sorry. No time."

He doesn't have enough time . . . for me.

Sigh.

But before he closed the door, he peeked his head back in and added, "Good night, Chicken."

Chicken. That's the name he always called me when I was a little kid. I loved it because Jason never had a nickname. We were just Jason and Chicken.

I almost called out to him so I could tell him about the Chevy's gift certificate. Almost. I just knew it would hurt too much to hear him say he didn't have time to go.

If I make it to the regional tournament though, Dad and I will finally have something to do together. It's the type of thing he CAN'T wiggle out of. Right?

Gotta sign off now, it's getting late. And even though I'm pretty tired and groggy, if my calculations are correct, we haven't seen each other in five days except for the fifty-two minutes of French class yesterday. But that doesn't count since it was in a different language.

We still have the shelter on Mondays. You're still planning on doing that, aren't you?

I can't wait for your birthday party. It's gonna be awesome . . . just you wait and see! Are we having spinach and pesto pizza (so yummy)? Please don't tell me you're still planning on only ordering pepperoni. Step it up—do something exotic!

Olivia

Grateful for:

1. Winning five chess games
2. Witnessing Ellie create a French-fry castle that could withstand a tsunami
3. Blinkie sitting on my lap while I watch YouTube
4. Jumbo-size Oreo Blizzards
5. Dad at least sticking his head back in one more time to call me Chicken—in a good way

Olivia,

Hey, sorry that we seem to be getting less than fifty minutes lately. I tried to find you after class yesterday, but I saw you walking away with Ellie. And I was going to wait for you today, but then Bethany had a note she needed to pass to me and we ended up walking to our lockers together.

Did I tell you Renee is going out with Travis now? They seem like a weird match, since you know how chatty Renee is and Travis always just sits there like a jar of paste.

Wait, have you met them yet?

So I'm writing this really fast during sixth period so I can drop off the notebook in your locker before we meet up tonight at the animal shelter. Seriously, how is it possible that I literally haven't seen you in over a week!

Yes, of course I'm still working at the shelter. I know we've both been so busy lately, but I'm not going to give up on Trigger. Or filing things for dogs like Trigger.

Anyway, that all sounds cool about Chess Club. I'm glad

you've found your people. Even if your people can be a little bit snobby, that's great that they are so nice to you. I'm sorry I can't invite Ellie to my birthday, though. I tried to get more people invited, but Mom said it's like fifteen dollars a person and they are already spending a fortune. It's a good thing I'm dropping the soap-opera angle—I would have to start a spin-off series with all the guests! And I don't really know her anyway.

Have your parents met her yet? Ellie sounds like your mom's cup of tea. (Although maybe not because her dad owns a Dairy Queen. Hopefully Ellie's mom is a football fan. Or from the South.) Maybe you guys can play doubles chess against them. Is that a thing? If not, I'm making it a thing. Tell your chess friends I invented a new game!

I never in a million years thought I would say this, but I'm starting to miss the Jackson Whittaker updates! We've spent three years dissecting every time you've breathed the same air as him, and now you TALK to him in class and it's

No Big Deal. Bethany abbreviates everything. Saves loads of time, trust me.

Shouldn't we be writing a script so you can talk to him at my birthday party instead of talking about a regional tournament? Isn't that why we started the clubs in the first place?

So I finally wrote my OIL—Official Invite List. I'll attach it in here. It sure took a while. And I have a BIG SURPRISE to give you tonight at the shelter! You are going to love it. I'm so excited, I feel like I'm that lady in *The Sound of Music*, spinning around and singing about all my favorite things. Tra-la-la!

Raindrops on roses and whiskers on kittens,

Piper

Grateful: one thing is enough. And I'll give it to you tonight!!

Birthday invite list . . .

1. YOU
2. Bethany Livingston
3. Tessa Ramsey
4. Eve Pinkler
5. Scarlet Kingborn
6. Joel Lamier
7. Ryan Dawson
8. Troy Addelson
9. Jackson Whittaker

10. Jordan Goldberg

11. Dana Huffington (she begged me!)

12. Andrea and Danny

13. Felicity from LARP!

14. Brittan Tanner (I need to come up with extra money because I'm over but I couldn't cut back.)

See? I don't have room for Ellie. But you'll have JACK-SON, so not worried about you a bit.

Piper,

You're right. I haven't even talked to you about Jackson! The fact that I was able to put words together in a sentence that even resembled normalcy is a huge feat for me, right?

I talked to Ellie and the other girls from Chess Club at lunch about him. They all think I'm ready to try another note to him. One that has his name on it so that it will land IN HIS HAND. I'll put one of the girls on alert to make sure Jordan isn't anywhere in the northern hemisphere when I give it to him.

I've been practicing what I'm going to write by jotting stuff down on my lunch napkin. It's starting to come together. Sort of.

And I can't wait to see you at the shelter tonight too. You have a surprise for me?? Well, guess what? I have a surprise for YOU!! Can't wait to show you.

Wheeeeeeee

—Olivia

Olivia?

Why are you late? Why aren't you here? I had my mom drop me off fifteen minutes early so I could see you! So I could give you . . . ta-da!

THIS INVITATION...

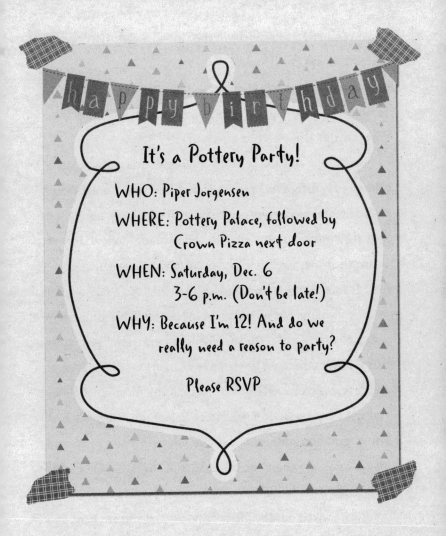

It's a Pottery Party!

WHO: Piper Jorgensen

WHERE: Pottery Palace, followed by
Crown Pizza next door

WHEN: Saturday, Dec. 6
3-6 p.m. (Don't be late!)

WHY: Because I'm 12! And do we
really need a reason to party?

Please RSVP

Isn't it just the most amazingest? I've never owned a piece of paper that is lovelier. Someday, I will pull aside my children, and my children's children, and say, "Come, my child. Come see the moment when your grandma, Nobel Peace

Prize Winner and President of the United States, first started her pathway to excellence."

"Grandma?" Little Henry will say (btw, he's also a piano prodigy or something. I'm going to have remarkable offspring). "Has anyone else seen this rare artifact?"

I will look out the window and smile wistfully. "Only a select few. Fourteen lucky peers, in fact. The Smithsonian asked to display this precious paper, but I declined. I believe one guest sold their invitation on eBay for one trillion dollars. I don't blame them. My twelfth birthday party was spectacular!"

My mom drove me around after school to pass them out. It was so much fun! She was so smart to have set the date nine days earlier than my real birthday. The first weekend of December isn't as busy as the rest. There aren't office parties or holiday choir concerts or cookie exchanges. It'll actually be about my birthday and not Christmassy! Plus, Pottery Palace was super booked. I'm so glad everything worked out. Oh, and when I dropped off Jackson's invitation, he asked IF YOU WERE GOING TO COME TOO. It's like all of our dreams are coming true.

I just looked out the office window and you are here! I'm going to GET ALL SCREAMY and start RanDomLy cApiTal-iZIng. And Miss Jill has us both cleaning out the file cabinet all afternoon, so we have loads of time to plan plan plan. So yeah. Invitation! Best surprise ever, right?

It's Time to Make the Right Move!

Kennedy Middle School is proud to support their team in the Central California Regional Chess Tournament!

Our players . . .
STEVE POLASKI
SARAH WASHINGTON
ANDREW BASKIN

And newcomer . . .
OLIVIA WESTON!!!

Date: SATURDAY, DEC. 6
Time: BEGINNING AT 2 P.M.

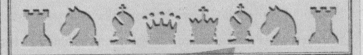

P—

I'm writing in This Notebook because I know once you get done fuming over there, you're going to be curious what I'm scribbling in here.

Piper. Why didn't you tell me you were doing your party so early? I just naturally figured it would be, like, on YOUR REAL BIRTHDAY. This regional tournament has been set since the beginning of the school year. The regional tournament doesn't care about when I joined or when you were born. The regional tournament is not going to be changed. And the regional tournament is what I will tell MY children and grandchildren about someday. Don't you get that? I worked hard and I earned this. I even beat out Ellie. She was named the alternate. I found her in the bathroom, rubbing at her eyes. I knew she was crying, but she claimed it was allergies. I feel awful for beating her since SHE'S the one who taught me everything. But she shook my hand, like a good friend.

I know those invitations are going to be worth a trillion

dollars someday, but can't you change the date? Imagine if I won, or placed, and my dad was sitting there watching me?

Everyone wants to come to your party. They'll make it happen.

Sliding this over to you. Talk to me.

0

Olivia,

So OTHER PEOPLE can make my party happen, but you aren't other people, right? No, you are part of the SPECIAL people, and special people put tournaments before best friends. Maybe you can have ELLIE go to the mall with you after. Go have TEA with your mom.

I know you do chess because it's important to feel close to your dad. But haven't you ever thought that this party is important to me because of my family too? There isn't ever anything that is just about me! I'm just the kid in the backseat driving around to everyone else's destinations. Designing and delivering those invitations with my mom was the first alone thing we've done in forever. Dad even helped us write the addresses out. Just the three of us at the kitchen table.

I'm not as different from you as you think.

And I'm so confused. You want me to drive to twelve other people's houses and de-invite them? What should I say? "Oh, sorry. This time doesn't work for Olivia. Chess is a priority."

We were so lucky to get into Pottery Palace. The only

opening they had for the next three Saturdays was that 3:00 p.m. slot, and my mom had to put down a one-hundred-dollar NONREFUNDABLE deposit. So should I also tell them to forget about the pottery part of the party? Should we all just come to your chess match?

You like lists. Let's think back to a very important list . . .

THE TWO REASONS WHY WE STARTED GOING TO CLUBS IN THE FIRST PLACE:

1. To Cast My Birthday. And I accomplished that. Sure, I never found an Ashley Desdemona, but I have a Bethany Livingston. The real-life people at our school are possibly better than the made-up people on my show.

2. Talk to Jackson Whittaker. Except you realized that talking to Jackson wasn't your problem. It was talking to anybody. Which is so true, Olivia. You clam up around people, and they never get to see the amazing person I do. Chess Club helped change that, but I'm worried it's changing you TOO much.

We agreed we wouldn't let anything or anyone come between us. We agreed we could make other friends as long as we stayed FOREVER friends. WE AGREED. But I'm not sure if that's happened. I think our tide pool ceremony didn't really work. I've branched out. You've branched out. But why does that have to mean we're branching AWAY from each other?

Going to the office to FILE.

Piper

Piper,

You forgot to add Danny on your goals.

　　—O

Olivia,

What are you talking about?

　　—Piper

P,

You also got to use LEGO Club as a way to see Danny. You had other good things happen too, so don't forget that. You said he acts weird in the hallway, but guess what? I saw you staring at him when you were at your locker the other day. Just staring.

　　O

Olivia,

Why would you possibly bring Danny into this? I don't care about Danny! I'm not the boy-crazy one here. STAY FOCUSED. I just shared my soul with you; write me back for real.

　　Piper

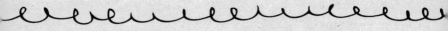

Piper,

OK, fine. I won't talk about Danny, even if I am totally right. But you notice everything about him—his lemonade stand, his braces-free teeth, everything. There's something going on there and you don't see it.

Just like how you've become friends with Savannah Swanson's crew when it hurts me. You don't see that either. I wish it didn't hurt, but it does. I want to think they're not so mean, but I don't even know *how* to give them a chance.

The thing is, I don't think you're being fair. Like AT ALL. You know what a big deal chess is to me and you know why. You don't know what it's like to suddenly be an only child and try to, like, win your parents' love when all they want to do is call Jason and talk about Jason and wonder about Jason and JasonJasonJason.

Your mom is so easygoing and your dad . . . your dad used to VOLUNTEER IN YOUR CLASSROOM. Remember? And then he stopped because you didn't like him reading with you in class because it made you nervous? I don't think my dad could name one teacher of mine. Ever. He knows the names of every ancient civilization and their modes of communication, but he can't even talk to me about why school gives me a stomachache.

You say that we have the same problems at home, but we don't. You don't understand what I'm going through. How could you?

Friendship is about sacrifice, and you haven't been doing that much for me lately. I haven't even seen you since you got all obsessed with being friends with everyone and their mom.

Are you jealous that I've gotten close to Ellie? Is that what this is really about?

I'm not going to apologize, Piper. That's what always happens. You get mad and I say I'm sorry, even if I'm not the one who was wrong. You should have asked me if that time worked before you scheduled it. Everything is always about YOU, and now there is something about ME, and I'm not sorry about it.

So . . . there.

Olivia

O—

Fine. Don't come to my party. There are ten other people who would love to come. And no, I'm not jealous of you. AT ALL. I've been super understanding and there for you for years. I'm the one who brought you a fake plant to cheer you up when those girls humiliated you. I'm ALWAYS cheering you up. And I didn't even TALK to the Savannah Swanson girls at first, even though they were nice to me. I was *trying* to be nice to you—cover your back, like *always*. But what happens? The first chance you get, you ditch me to shove a horsey thing across a checkerboard.

I'm going to call my mom and have her come pick me up early. And don't tell me I don't understand what it's like to be in your shoes. Feeling alone is feeling alone. Sympathy is sympathy. Parents are parents, Olivia. At least you don't have a sibling around anymore getting in the way! (Okay. Not that I think my siblings get in the way. You were just being super only-childy there. AND YOU AREN'T EVEN AN ONLY CHILD!)

P—

Fine. I won't come, and I don't even feel bad. I'll probably go to Dairy Queen after with my friends and have best time ever! That's real mature to leave the animal shelter IN NEED because you're mad at me. Here, take the notebook.

O—

Keep the notebook.

Don't bother writing me anything else.

I won't read it.

Have a nice CHESS-FILLED life!

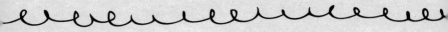

Piper,

Two days. We've had two days of silence.

But you know what? I have things I want to say and this is the only way I know how to tell you. I know you won't read this. And it doesn't even matter.

It's strange how I thought this notebook was going to be the thing that kept us together . . . the thing that would be our lifeline. But all it did was tear us apart.

You have a whole new world now. Friends. Popularity. A super-long party-invite list.

And you're just . . . gone.

Honestly, I'm glad you're gone. You deserve your paper-thin friendships. You'd rather throw some attention-seeking bash just to put on a spectacular show than spend a boring night watching me play a chess tournament.

Guess what? Life isn't a soap opera, Piper. So why are you always trying to make it one?

Why couldn't you have postponed the party? Don't you see that I've finally found MY thing? That Chess Club is the place where I truly feel like myself? I don't even feel like myself around you anymore.

I hope you enjoy your pottery and your new friends. Or friends who are acting like friends. Just don't come running to me when they all ignore you once this party is over. That's what people like them do to other people. They act like they're your friend and then set you up for humiliation the next chance they get. They're just the same as Savannah Swanson and those girls in third grade. JUST THE SAME. I mean, some of those ARE the same because they were WITH Savannah!

Don't come looking for me when they aren't there anymore. I'm not going to be there for you either.

I would end this with a grateful, but right now, I can't think of anything I'd want to share with you.

And that makes me sadder than you'll ever know.

Olivia

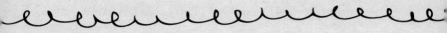

Piper,

Whether you ever read this or not, just know that my life is crumbling. My life is a Girl Scout shortbread cookie.

You know that letter to Jackson? The one I've been writing on my lunch napkin? The one Ellie and her friends are helping me with?

It's.

Terrible.

They want me to make jokes. Actual knock-knock jokes. That's their idea of flirting.

I have no idea what to say to him. That's always been your department. You always have the best suggestions, the best ideas. But now your department doesn't exist.

This isn't easy. It's just not.

—Olivia

Here's the lame letter they want me to give him. Not that you'll even see this.

Jackson,
Knock knock!
Who's there?
To who?
No, no . . . to WHOM.

Hope you liked my joke! But I have one
question . . . how is it that I know so many
hundreds of digits of pi, but not the seven digits
of your phone number?

               —Olivia

My life is crumbling.

Piper,

It's pretty late. I'm leaning against my bed, the way you and I always did when we had late-overs and we'd write out our favorite playlists—the ones we wanted to play at our wedding because we just KNEW we'd have a double wedding. Pink with purple/orange/aqua accents. Rainbow-striped veils. The wedding planner threatening to sue the DJ for breaking her heart.

I'm not sure why I'm thinking about all of that.

I guess because I was listening to Track 1 of our playlist and it hit me that our double wedding will never happen. We can't even agree on flowers.

(Deep, calming breath . . .)

How did this happen?
—Liv

(This page is my soul, Piper.)

(Empty.)

Hi, Mrs. Jorgensen. It's Olivia. Could you get a message to Piper for me?

Sure, honey. Whatcha need?

Could you let her know I hope she has a great party?

Of course. We will miss having you there, sweetie.

And I'm really sorry I can't go. I wish I could go. Would you tell her?

Sure. Have to go check on twins now. Good night!

What did you end up ordering for the pizza? Pepperoni, I'm guessing? Or did she branch out and get spinach and pesto?

Liv, why don't you just call Piper?

We're not talking.

Should I ask why?

It's a lot of things really. Probably a lot more things than a text should handle.

I will have a talk with Piper. Good night . . .

And did you get her any yellow balloons?

Hello? Okay. Bye.

Liv,

It's Friday. And it rained this week. So can we meet at our tide pool today? I think I'm getting those weird stomachaches you get about my party. At least I think it's about my party.

—Piper

★ BETHANY'S BUSINESS ❤

HOME   NEWS   EVENTS   ABOUT   CONTACT

Holy hippopotamus! I know I said last weekend was the best, and at the time it was, but then this weekend happened and ruined all other weekends for me forever.

I'm totally getting ahead of myself. First, let me give my Sunday stats:

3 = number of people I complimented today

6:40 = Time I woke up so I could curl my hair

8:25 = How fast I ran the mile in track!

12th = My reading level! I just finished the last *Lord of the Rings* and now I think I'm going to start some of the Russian novelists. Dad said those are SUPER long and hard ☺

1 gazillion = The number of times my mom complained about the literacy curriculum at our school

239

AND NOW IT'S TIME FOR SOME KUDOS!!

★ Tessa, who had on the CUTEST reindeer sweater today. I want to steal ALL OF HER CLOTHES.

★ Tennis team for winning against the Bayside Turtles, which is, like, the lamest mascot. Sorry, Bayside.

★ Our choir gets to sing songs from *FROZEN*! Oh my gosh, I know those songs by heart, and I hope hope hope I get a solo. Although I'll be happy for whoever gets it.

★ Oh, and I guess there was some sort of math thing and a chess tournament, and . . . I don't know what else. I don't know where I put my school newsletter. But yay everyone for doing your thing!

So back to my weekend. Friday night was cool. My parents took me to this uber fancy steakhouse and I got to order a lobster tail, and even though I think fish is pretty gross, I loved ordering it. And I wore my adorable pink sequin dress from my aunt Catherine's wedding.

And then Saturday was Piper Jorgensen's birthday party. Piper is that girl who goes to my church and stuck up for Tessa at LEGO Club.

She always seemed kind of . . . like she just wanted to do her own thing before. But now we are, like, WAY close and I love her bunches! She's really, really funny. Anyway, she invited twelve people cuz she's twelve. And then two or three more because she's so so popular. AND THERE WERE BOYS. It was the first guy/girl party my parents let me go to. Not that it was advertised as one. Like we didn't dance or kiss each other or anything. But my parents are usually so strict about it, and they didn't even care that there were boys there! And there is one boy I kind of like, WHO I WON'T NAME, but his name starts with a J. Anyway, we sat by each other during the pottery part. We all got to choose a different ceramic thing, and I heard J say that he loves to drink tea, and although I thought that was kind of gross and weird, since he's twelve, I decided to be super brave and make him a tea MUG. Which is a coffee mug for tea.

Ugh, but here is the bad part. He started talking about another girl.

"Hey, is everyone here already?" he asked me as he smeared more black on his dragon figurine.

"I don't know exactly who RSVPed," I said helpfully. "But we're twenty minutes in, so anyone with good manners would be here by now."

"Huh. What about that Olivia girl?"

"Who?"

"You know. Piper's best friend."

"Oh yeah. I don't know." Note: I really didn't know. It's hard to keep track of every single person at the school. I think Piper mentioned her before, but I haven't met her. Hi, Olivia, if you're reading this!

J frowned. "I totally came because I wanted to see her."

Right. So this was the NOT AWESOME part of
the day.

But then Tessa said, "Don't bother. She's in love
with Jackson."

"Seriously?" Jordan . . . I mean, J asked. "Are you
sure?"

"Positive!" I said. "So, anyway, you like tea, right?"

And then we just started to chat up a storm!! And
I got so brave and painted TO JORDAN on the
bottom of the coffee . . . sorry, tea mug (duh, there's
no reason not to just write his name here. If he's
reading this, he knows who he is ☺).

So then we were cleaning up and this girl in a
super-cute A-line skirt rushed in with some old guy
and Piper started crying and they were hugging and
blabbering and hugging. We were supposed to go
to the pizza place then, but stayed a little longer so
that girl could work on her jewelry jar. Jackson went

and sat by her, and that kind of made Jordan talk to me more, so I didn't mind.

And then we went to Crown Pizza, and some kids from our school who weren't even invited showed up, so then there were over twenty of us, and we had a skeeball tournament and the boys did a basketball competition on that moving hoop game. Jordan bought me some cotton candy with his tickets too.

Seriously, best party ever. I'm so glad Piper and I are friends!

It's so late, and I still have to practice violin AND start reading *The Scarlet Letter*, since that's on the ninth grade required reading list and I already blew through the middle school reads.

Thanks for reading, peeps! Tell me in comments what YOU did this weekend.

6 COMMENTS

Tammi35: OMG, I wish I'd gotten invited to that party! Sounds awesome!

Davedude: Played Minecraft, watched YouTube videos of people playing Minecraft. Creepers, yo!

Danahuffhuff: The party was so awesome. But wait. What if Jordan reads this? LOL.

Ellieheartschess: I'm pretty sure the girl in the A-line skirt WAS Olivia. I'm glad everything worked out. Your blog is awesomesauce.

Vitaminsdirect: Excellent post! You can find out more about my life-changing vitamins by going directly to my blog and paying $19.95....

Bethanyblogs: Spammers? Seriously? Managing this blog is like a full-time job. I need an intern.

O. L. I. V. I. A.

Hello, best friend,

I did read all of your letters in here. Let's not talk about the first one. And we don't even need to talk about the Jackson one because, well, I think that worked out at my party. ☺ Also, I found the Post-It note I wrote you under a locker a few doors down from you. I went back to check if you got it, and there it was, smooshed underneath. I put it in The Notebook and I included the text conversation you had with my mom that I didn't even see! For the sake of historical accuracy.

But I'm TOTALLY getting ahead of myself.

I printed off Bethany's blog post to document my party from some different points of view. (Again. Historical accuracy. You're welcome, aliens.) I'm glad my party was such a hit, but more than anything I'm so glad *you* came. I think you're a little right—the party sort of took over my life for a while! And it wasn't about being soap opera-y (even though it was!). The party became more about (See! I'm list-ing like you. BFF.):

1. My parents doing something just for me. Which I always said didn't matter, but I think when we started writing our feelings about family stuff in this notebook, I realized it DID matter. And at my party my dad said he was glad to do something "just for me" because I'm always doing stuff for other people. And he said that's why I made friends so easily when I finally wanted to. Because I'm good at helping out. That whole conversation was almost better than the new yarn I got as a b-day gift!

2. I think that's part of why I do like having friends now. Even though it takes work and I still like being close with just a few people (and soap operas), reaching out to people was . . . well, it was fun, okay? There, I said it. Tell Bethany Livingston and you die. I love the girl, but I still have to take her exclamation points in small doses.

Olivia, when you weren't there . . . I mean, we might as well have had Disneyland all to ourselves and I wouldn't have been happy. All day Saturday I was SO SICK. I was worried I would have to cancel the party. My mom said it was nerves, but I've never had that before. I just started thinking about who I would sit by while we were painting and what we would talk about. And suddenly I almost wished my birthday would be completely different. I even started to think it might be more fun to just do a night at a neat restaurant with you and tell my parents to save the money. Which was such a practical, non-dramatic thought (well, except for the deposit my parents would have lost), I almost got sick again. Ashley Desdemona would cry into her scarf if she ever heard such normal-person talk.

We got to the party thirty minutes early. I scoped out the different pottery choices, but nothing called to me, even the owl cookie jar I'd been longing for. Whatever I painted would go on the shelf and I would look at it and think, "That's from my twelfth birthday." And what if my party ended up being a bust and no one came, or I mixed the colors wrong and my owl or unicorn or narwhal ended up a sad muddy brown?

So I went with a bowl. I decided I'd paint it blue. Seemed like the least dangerous option.

Bethany and Tessa got there five minutes early. Apparently, Bethany is a big believer in being punctual. Dang, they are peppy. Tessa kept flipping her hair. I thought she might knock over a vase with it. Then no one came for seventeen minutes. Yes, that's exact. It was excruciating. No one told me about that part of party planning—the waiting-for-everyone-to-get-there angst. Can you imagine if NO ONE came after all I'd been through—after all *we've* been through?

But they did. And I think they were all having a good time—I mean, that's what Bethany's blog said. And there I was, painting my blue bowl bluer, and feeling guilty because my parents had spent all this money and time so I could finally have a party, and I wasn't even having fun.

"What's wrong?" Mom asked me when I left the table to find some indigo to swirl into the azure.

"Nothing! This party is so fun! Thanks so much, Mom!"

My mom actually winced. "Why are you using so many exclamation points?"

"Sorry, sometimes that happens when I've been around Bethany for a while."

Mom patted my back. "Olivia really wanted to be here."

"How do you know?" I grumbled. Remember, we still weren't talking at this point. So I was in grumbling mode.

"She texted last night."

I almost dropped my paint. "She what? Why are you just telling me this NOW?!"

Mom shrugged. "Honestly, I forgot. You were in bed—"

"Whatdidshesay?!"

Mom pulled out her phone and showed me the text

conversation. Then she pushed some hair away from my face. "Piper, I just want you to have a good time and be happy. I thought doing this big party would be your thing, since you have so many friends."

"I don't have so many friends," I said automatically. "Most of these people weren't even my friends until last month."

Mom looked confused. "You mean, you made all these friends FOR the party?"

"Well . . . yeah. The more the merrier—well, more dramatic."

"Oh, honey, you weren't trying to make this one of your soaps, were you?"

"No! Sort of." Um . . . make sure my mom never finds my Casting Sheet, okay? "Not a big episode—if things got too dramatic, then all this pottery would get smashed."

Mom sighed. "So do you know these kids?"

"Oh, totally. I mean, the church girls I already knew. But we weren't close or anything. Usually, it's just me and Olivia."

"I bet that's hard not having her here then." Mom patted my back. I love/hate when she does that, because it's clear I need it.

It was hard, Olivia! SO SO HARD. And I felt so stupid, because it was, like, in that moment that I realized how grateful I was to have you. There were all these fun, nice people at my party. And I'm really glad I got to know them better, because I think I can really be friends with them all in my big ecosystem of life, yada yada.

But they aren't you. Somewhere along the way, I forgot how wonderful OUR friendship is. I mean, so you missed my party (initially) for a chess tournament. So what? There are loads of birthday parties in our future! We're having a combined fortieth birthday party someday! I'm sure we'll both have lots of friends, but that's not going to take away from what we have.

All of this is all to say . . . that's why I stopped off at your house on the way to the party. Your dad said you were busy getting ready. I wish we could've talked before your tournament, but he promised to give you the surprise I left. He even smiled.

Anyway, back to the party . . . at this point, I had somehow swirled my blue bowl into a sad brown. I asked Mom if I could do another pottery project if I did it myself, and Mom winked and said, "You're the birthday girl. Do two."

I really do have amazing parents, and not just because they sometimes buy me stuff. They let me do mostly what I want and they're there when I need them. Just thought I should mention that.

So then the door opened, and I hoped it was you, but no. It was Danny Moss, and Andrea, who I invited because we talked about the party the last time I babysat her. And I like her and I don't care if she's nine. Tessa spotted Danny so she got up and moved to a faraway table, which was not that mature, but whatever.

Danny scooped up his skateboard and tucked it under his arm so he wouldn't knock anything over. "Hey, Piper. Happy birthday."

"Thanks!" Okay, so not only was he NOT being rude, but now he was being nice. I really don't know what to do about this boy, Olivia.

Andrea gave me a hug. "I'm thinking of painting a lion. Don't you think a lion would be a good addition to the deserted island storyline we're doing?"

Um. Yeah. I've kind of taught Andrea some LARP techniques with . . . uh . . . her toys. And we've maybe made some videos of it. Like, seven videos. They're pretty popular online, but don't tell anyone about it.

Andrea went off to find a good lion, and then Danny just stood there. "So, uh . . . should I pick her up at six then?"

"Yep. I bet there are some great places to skateboard around here until then."

"Oh." Danny shrugged. "Okay."

Maybe I'm not as good at sarcasm as I thought, because sometimes people really miss it. "I'm kidding, Danny! Didn't you see I put your name on the invitation too?"

"For real?" Danny actually smiled. I've never see him

smile, besides his selling-stuff smile, or being-mean smile. His real-life smile was sort of nice.

I have to admit . . . you were right. I do notice things about him. This is all so weird. And if you tell anyone I will deny, deny, deny.

"Even with Tessa around?" Danny asked.

I glanced behind me. "Tessa already moved so she doesn't get your germs. Besides, you're here to help your sister. You're kind of stuck. And I don't mind a little drama at my party." Understatement, right? You know, Danny actually reminds me of Brett McArthur, the friendly but sharp-tongued fire-fighter from season four of *Love and Deception*. Did I just use the word "friendly"? Oh, boy. I guess he's starting to become a friend. Again, this is all so weird.

Danny picked up a big spaghetti bowl. "It would be kind of cool if I made something for my mom for Christmas."

Which was oddly sweet. But anyway, I don't know why I spent all these notebook lines telling you about Danny. He did help me pick out the jewelry box. One heart broken in half with "Best friends" on it! So perfect. At this point, I already knew I didn't hate you and that giving you the jewelry box would be the best way to try and make up with you when . . . (you know this part!)

YOU SHOWED UP!!!!

WOO-TO-THE-HOO, ✳ ✳ ✳ BABY! ✳ ✳ ✳

And that was the best present of the whole party, Olivia. Really, one of the best presents of my life. After that, my party was amazing. Not that I even cared about the party at that point, because we were just having so much fun, like we always do, and that's what matters.

Sorry your half of the best-friend heart I made you turned out a little brown. Don't think that's a metaphor or anything. I'm just a really lousy painter. Next party, we're doing LASER TAG instead. ☺

Now, we still need to cover what happened at Crown Pizza (because we agreed we need an accurate record for after all human life is over). But I think I have a really good idea how to do that.

<3,

Piper

Grateful: the color brown, Danny being nice, YOU AT MY PARTY, my parents being so awesome, and being featured in Bethany's blog. Again. Are we famous or what?

SPEEDING TICKET

104 043 6305

PERPETRATOR
Ted Weston

LICENSE
XLG9758

OFFICER NAME
Danville, R.

CHARGE
Exceeding maximum speed: 45 miles per hour in a residential 25 mph zone

CODE F.46

OFFENSE DATE Dec. 6.   **TIME** 3:18 p.m.

NOTES

Defendant agreeable to officer's requests. Defendant's wife explained the excess in speed was due to a party they needed to get to because they were late. Wife requested an escort. Request denied.

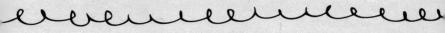

Piper,

I can't believe we made it on time. Or almost on time. There were a few hurdles in our way, as you see now with this ticket Dad got. I was fairly sure Officer Danville was going to throw us in jail when Mom demanded we get a police escort instead of a ticket. Dad had to do a lot of "Yes, Officer, in the future we will make it to a kid's birthday party without police intervention."

Yep. Dad sped through a neighborhood just to get me to Pottery Palace in time to find you. Dad never speeds. He never even fast-forwards TV programs.

That's how much my parents wanted to make sure I got there.

Here's why . . .

We were on our way to the chess tournament. I was in the backseat, where I should have been bouncing my knees, giddy as ever. I should have been happy that the night before, my dad had come to check in on me and said, "I'm excited about tomorrow."

I should have been beaming as I sat in that backseat.

But I wasn't. I was biting at my lower lip to stop it from quivering. And Dad kept sitting forward to get a glimpse of me in his rearview mirror. I did my best to stare out the window and hope he didn't ask questions.

Except when he pulled up to the convention center where the tournament was being held, I saw the sign outside. "Welcome Kennedy Middle School Chess Team." And by the time my dad had pulled the car into park, my eyes started to well up with tears.

You won't believe it, but it was my mom who turned around first. She even put her hand on top of mine. "What's wrong, Liv?"

"I . . . I . . ." I couldn't talk. I was too busy wiping the snot away. Sorry for the TMI.

Dad turned all the way around to face me. "You're not worried about the competition, are you?"

Sniffle, sniffle. "I'm at the wrong place—"

"Oh, no. Did I read the directions wrong?" He scrolled through his phone, looking at the map.

"No, Dad. I think I made the wrong choice. And now I don't know how to fix it."

Mom patted my hand. "You can tell us."

"Piper's birthday party. It's at the Pottery Palace and then they're having pizza. It's a big deal. But I told her I had to come to this chess tournament. I thought this chess tournament would fix everything. . . ."

Dad tilted his head at me. "Fix what?"

Boy, did I ever do the deepest, most cleansing breath ever. Preparing to tell your dad the truth requires lots of oxygen. That's when Mom squeezed my hand. I looked up at her and saw that her eyes had softened. She didn't say any words, but that look she gave me . . . wow. It was like she finally understood why I was sad. I'd been waiting so long for one of those dramatic moments like the ones in the movies where I unload my feelings on my parents and they just . . . get it.

It happened, Piper—right there in the backseat of my dad's Ford.

One more quick breath and I said it. "Dad, I did this— joined a chess club and made it to this tournament . . . just so you'd go with me. So we could have something to do together. I ended up making some friends and it's been great. But the reason I joined in the first place was so maybe you'd stop thinking about Jason for a minute and—"

He rubbed his temple. "You mean you did this . . . for me?"

Wipe, sniffle, wipe. "Yeah." I pressed my forehead against the window and added in a soft voice, "I just wanted you to be proud."

He reached back over the car seat and grabbed my hand. Both of my parents were now holding my hands, if you're keeping count. BOTH OF THEM. "I am proud, Chicken. I always have been." He squeezed my hand harder.

I flashed him a little grin. He'd called me Chicken.

I know you'll get what a huge thing that was. I know you feel like it's so hard to get your parents to pay attention to you sometimes. Different situation. But totally the same feelings. And I love that about our friendship, more than anything— that you get me too.

But then Dad's smile faded into a frown. "Oh, no. I forgot to tell you something."

I sat up straight. "Tell me what?"

"Piper came by the house. She had a surprise to give you, but I told her you were busy. You were doing that nervous pacing thing, and I know how you don't like people seeing you doing your nervous pacing thing."

He was right, and it kind of made my insides twitch with joy that he remembered my nervous pacing thing. But for you I would've made an exception. Dad didn't know that, though.

I leaned forward in my seat. "What did she bring me?"

He raised a brow. "A flower. An orchid—a fake one. She said you'd know what it meant."

I pressed my lips together, hoping I could stop from

crying. But tears flowed down my face. I turned into a snot river.

(TMI again?)

"A fake potted plant?" my mom said. "Couldn't she get you a fresh bouquet from the farmer's market?"

Mom had no idea how much that fake plant meant to me. But my dad, on the other hand . . .

"So if you want to know what I think?" Dad said with a smile. "I think you're right. We're in the wrong place."

My face lit up. "Do you mean I can go to the party?"

"There is the issue of you letting your team down, though," Dad said.

I reached for the door handle. "No, there's not, actually. There's someone much more deserving of my spot on the team. I have to get in there and find Ellie. She's the one who really deserves this."

Dad shot me a sneaky grin. "Then go. Tell her to take your place. We have a party to get to!"

I sprinted inside the building to find Ellie. The guys were already pacing backstage going over chess moves, but there was no Ellie. The bathroom—that was the only place she could be.

And yep, she was hanging out in the last stall, stress-eating a bag of Cheetos with tears in her eyes. "Take my place. You're the one who's been in the club since the beginning. You taught me all the things I know. And I don't even want to be here. Will you please play for me?"

She had just stuffed a bunch of Cheetos in her mouth. "Weally??" And then she smothered me with a hug. But when she stepped back, we realized she had smeared Cheeto dust all over her shirt. "I can't go out there with this streaked orange shirt."

Being someone who had cried in a bathroom with a bag of Cheetos before, I knew exactly how that felt. "Take mine." So we switched shirts. She ran out there wearing a sharp-looking blouse with ruffled sleeves, and I sprinted back out to the parking lot looking like a streaky orange monster.

"We have to stop by the house first. Quick change!"

Mom, of course, was all in favor of this. "Step on it. No daughter of mine is going to an important pottery party without a crisp clean shirt. Or maybe we could just swing by a department store to find something—"

"No time!" Dad and I both yelled.

So that's why we got a ticket in a residential area. And that's why I showed up in my favorite Christmas Eve blouse. (It was the only one I could find that was pressed and ready to go on such short notice. Also, I didn't look around all that much. I HAD TO GET TO A PARTY!)

I'm glad I made it almost on time, at least before the party had moved on to Crown Pizza. And I'm sorry I tried to go to some stupid chess tournament instead of your once-in-a-lifetime party event. Which it WAS. Even Tessa and Eve were nice to me. It was as if the third grade incident had never happened.

Sitting there next to those girls made me realize that I hadn't joined those clubs just to talk to Jackson.

It wasn't about the guy.

It was about moving on . . . breaking away from third grade me and becoming the NOW me.

Does that make sense? It's all sort of starting to make sense to me now. It's about time, I guess.

So your muddy-colored heart jewelry box was perfect. Guess what? Brown is my go-to color when I'm lonely and missing my best friend.

I wasn't sure if you were missing me all that time that we weren't talking to each other, but now I'm glad I know you did.

So I guess there's really only one thing left to say:

HAPPY BIRTHDAY, PIPER.

It was awesome.

But wait . . . you have a plan for how to talk about Crown Pizza and that whole thing with Jackson? I'm lifting my brow at you . . . I'm very curious. . . .

I have a feeling it's time to pop some popcorn.

Olivia

♥ PIPER & OLIVIA'S ♥
SUPER FUN SLUMBER
PARTY ATTEMPT
AT A LARP

Setting: Crown Pizza

(No, Olivia, it's supposed to be fiction. So call it Dragon Lairs of Evil Ninjas . . . Palace.)

Seriously?

Yes. Remember, I'm the Game Master and experienced LARPer. Please trust me as I introduce you to this magical world.

Yawn. Wow. I'm sort of tired. Maybe I'll get my jammies on and get to bed.

No! This is the number-one activity of our slumber party. The fact that your parents are letting you spend the ENTIRE night is a modern miracle. That means NO SLEEPING. Besides, I played chess with you!

Played isn't really the word I would use . . .

CAST:

Orc—Jordan

Ninja Prince—Jackson

Birthday President of the World—Piper

(What does that have to do with warriors?)

(Nothing, but it's my birthday. I can be what I want, right?)

Rook—Olivia

(Wait, what's a rook again?)

(The horsey thing, sweetie. And yes, that was sarcasm. The horsey thing looks like a horse and is actually called a knight. The rook looks like a castle-y thing.)

They are playing skeeball, I mean . . . throwing a gauntlet? Or whatever warriors do. That's what we're all doing.

Good job. I can tell you're already getting into the inner mind of your character!

THE SCRIPT:

BIRTHDAY PRESIDENT OF THE WORLD (*having so much fun, giggling*): Methinks this is the noblest birthday party I've doth ever seen! Hey, did I tell you Danny gave me a coupon to his lemonade stand? For a birthday present? I don't know if he's being nice or it's a joke.

He came and stayed, right? I think he was being nice.

Your hair looked great, by the way. No wonder he stayed. *wink*

I don't LIKE him, if that's what you're saying.

I didn't say that. You just did.

Well, I don't.

Of course you don't. Who are we talking about again?

Dan . . . funny. Yeah. Exactly.

BPOTW: Okay, sorry. Back to the Dragon Lair . . . We live in dangerous times, even amidst this jubilation! You never know what is lurking in the shadows. . . .

Wow. You're really getting into this.

ROOK: Oh . . . my! I see a Ninja Warrior Guy. And he has one of those balls and chains with spikes on it, what are those called?

BPOTW: Balls and chains with spikes on it.

NINJA PRINCE: Hey, girls. Skeeball's cool.

ROOK: I just got a high score.

NINJA: Cool.

ROOK: I saw you playing basketball.

NINJA: Yeah.

ROOK: You like playing basketball? You're good at lots of sports, right?

NINJA: I guess.

(*awkward pause, but not too awkward*)

(YAWN. Is this a direct retelling of your conversation?)

(Yeah? So?)

(Er . . . nothing. Carry on.)

NINJA: You're pretty good at math.

ROOK: Yeah, I guess.

NINJA: I'm not so great at it. We should meet up for tutoring sometime.

ROOK: Totally. I could totally do that.

(*The president GRABS horsey by the mane and tries not rip her hair out with excitement.*)

Seriously, Piper. I have bruises from all your poking and nudging! And rooks have no mane, no—forget it. Not important.

But look above. Do you see what I see? A FULL CONVERSATION WITH JACKSON. Where you initiated most of the talking. And then HE brought up the tutoring, which was our initial plan. Bam! Boom! The peasants rejoiced!!

I know! And I wasn't even nervous. It all just came . . . natural to me. I think talking to all those new people at Chess Club gave me a little more warrior spirit.

And kingdoms fell, children wept, for the fair horse had

climbed the highest mountain and . . .

Come back to earth. Then stupid warrior guy I didn't even know—

Travis.

Whatever. Thanks for inviting him.

I didn't invite him. He crashed my party. PEOPLE CRASHED MY PARTY.

Anyway, Travis the stupid warrior grabbed Jackson to go into battle/play a game of air hockey.

And lo, how we rejoiced!!!

Settle down. We get it, Piper. THE END.

NO! Not the end. You forgot the part where the drooly Orc offered you jewels, no one knows what in exchange for, perhaps for pittance upon his people.

You mean when Jordan came over and gave me his tokens because he had to leave?

That's the boring way to say it, but yes. And he was nice and funny and you guys talked for three whole minutes.

I know. He didn't act like I'm in love with him anymore. So he isn't all that bad, just being a nice guy. A really nice guy.

That's what all the Orcs want you to think.

Are we done now?

And the maidens rejoiced! Because despite all the ninjas, Orcs, lemonade sellers, tournaments, clubs, and stupid fights in their lives, they still had each other.

And THAT is truly the greatest treasure of all the land!

OLIVIA AND PIPER'S DOUBLE GRATEFUL LIST!

Olivia—the brown color of my half of the heart on the box
Piper—and the purple color of mine

Olivia—the fact that Bethany blogged about YOUR party
Piper—and there were seven comments, not counting the three that I wrote and then deleted

Olivia—my dad willing to speed through a residential area
Piper—AND talking smack to that cop! Or not smack, but enough agreeing to get you to my party

Olivia—spinach and pesto pizza
Piper—PUH-LEEZ! Pepperoni. But only on takeout Tuesday when it's cheaper

Olivia—that there are more pages left in this notebook
Piper—LOTS of pages ☺

Acknowledgments

Robin,

Girl. GIRL. Remember that time you sent me a quick, vague message that said, "I have a proposition for you?" (That's not a direct quote. I tried to find the message but you know how organized I am with email. Translation: not organized.) Anyway, curiosity and my deep desire to become your best friend led me to a phone call, which led to some emailing, "work" that never felt like work, "business trips" involving excessive snacks, and now . . . here we are. We co-wrote a book! You are brilliant, tenacious, strong and kind. So I would like to start off by acknowledging YOU and your great idea and your greater idea to include me. EveRYtHinG iS AweSoMe BECausE of YOU!!

> I'm obsessed with you,
> Lindsey

Lindsey,

Girl. GIRL. I can't believe a phone call that started with "Wouldn't it be fun if . . ." led to this. A BOOK. Writing this with you was so much fun. Almost TOO much fun? But I must admit something to you: this was all just an elaborate hoax to force you into best friendship with me. And it worked! (Insert maniacal laughter here.) Anyway, this is the "acknowledgment" section so I will now acknowledge YOU for being hysterical, supportive, flexible (physically not emotionally—I'm kidding), and all-around AWESOME.

I also want to acknowledge a few other people in my life who help make this writing gig possible: Jill, Jayson, Luke, my parents, and chocolate.

Oh! And there's one person in particular that we need to give a giant BFF hug to . . . our editor, Kristen Pettit. She helped us find the sparkle inside Piper and Olivia and we are so fortunate for her guidance. She is WonDerFuL, amirite?!

Write me back, bestie . . .

Robin

Robin,

Absolutely. Kristen Pettit puts the Won in WonDerFuL. She's sharp, smart, and her sense of humor is basically the same as ours, so of course we love her. Everyone at HarperCollins has been lovely. Thank you Elizabeth Lynch, Jessica Berg, Allison Brown, Jessica Gould, Sarah Creech, Christina Colangelo, Kate Jackson, Susan Katz, and Jen Klonsky. Snickerdoodles for every single one of you! (But not real snickerdoodles. Because we don't want to get cinnamon on the pages.)

Lindsey

Lindsey,

AND TUESDAY MOURNING! How did we get so lucky to have the incredibly talented TUESDAY MOURNING illustrate the cover of our book? Tuesday, Tuesday, we adore you!

Robin

Robin,

Thank you also to Sarah Davies, for your charm, class, and British accent. The accent can't be helped, but it's always a bonus. My parents, Eric and Carol, for All The Things, big and small. My generous siblings, my patient friends, my noble gentleman caller, and especially Sheridan Garhett and Paige Bledsoe for help with the girlies.

Ahhh. My girlies. Rylee, Talin, & Logan. You are sunshine and goodness. The world is wide-open. Tie up your shoes and chase after those dreams. Also, put on your seat belt. Don't look at me like that. I can tell when it's off.

ARGH, I always cry when I write these things. Remind me to give you an extra hug when I see you next, Robbie.

(Note: I have never called you Robbie. But maybe we should have secret code names?)

LindA(sey) ((CODE NAME))

LindA,

Why did you have to mention snickerdoodles? Now I'm going to go bake. And as soon as I get these cookies done, guess what we're going to do?

Robbie

R-

Write some more letters?

—L

L-

I can't imagine a better way to spend the day. Ready? Check your inbox . . . ☺

R

Find out what happens next!

Piper,

You. Me. This top secret notebook. Together again! Finally!!

It felt like winter break lasted forever, but in a mere nine hours, forty-three minutes, we will be walking through the doors of Kennedy Middle School, where every student will be sporting brand-new itchy sweaters. Yay! (I think.)

The plan will be the same—we'll drop off the notebook in our lockers and exchange it in the hallway between classes. Let's document every step of the way for fun. Or as my dad, the Coolest Anthropologist in California, would say, "For anthropology's sake!"

Our wise words could educate the little green aliens when they someday beam down here. (Or do aliens beam *up* here? Come on, scientists. We need answers!) Not that aliens should read this since we made it very clear this notebook is off-limits.

These are our secrets.

Our precious thoughts.

Our "only my best friend will understand" letters.

Perhaps we should have made it clear to the aliens . . . "Do not read even if you're not a human and from the future."

It's possible aliens-from-the-future will be very gossipy.

Also, the Martians could steal all our amazing double wedding ideas, and suddenly everyone will have six-foot-long banana splits at their reception, and our original idea won't be original anymore.

Stay on your own planet, please.

So here I am sitting on my bed staring at Blinkie as I wait for school to start. He's meowing a lot tonight. Maybe he's nervous for me.

Am I nervous? Hold on.

I just asked Blinkie. He blinked twice.

As we all know, my cat blinks once for YES, twice for NO.

And guess what! He's right—I'm *not* nervous. Which is practically headline news. You know how I get when I have to deal with change—it turns my stomach into a knot. The tricky kind of knot you have to learn for a Girl Scout badge. Usually going back to school puts me in Full Worried Mode.

What if it's too warm inside to wear this sweater and I, you know . . . sweat?

What if headbands suddenly went out of style over the holidays?

What if I'm assigned a report that has to be read out loud . . . in front of PEOPLE?

But that's the *old* me; even more specifically, it's December me. *January* me has decided to take charge of her life.

Be bold.

Be fearless.

No, I didn't read any self-help books over winter break. It's better than that!

Remember when I told you I started having lunch in Ms. Benson's office once a week? Well, it's supposed to be a friendly chat, but she's been using her guidance counselor skills on me. I can tell. My guess is once you get your counseling degree, you can't really turn it off, lunchtime or not.

Anyway, lately she's been giving me strategies to deal with anxiety. But I don't like calling it anxiety (because that word makes me . . . anxious). I call it Worry Wort Syndrome (WWS), which is a more accurate description of me. Or it was.

Ms. Benson told me all about this thing called "catastrophic thinking," which is figuring out the worst thing that could happen and then letting that thought bounce around in your head until you almost convince yourself that awful thing will definitely happen.

She says I'm supposed to question my thoughts like I'm some sort of detective getting to the facts. During our last meeting, we examined my catastrophic thinking about not giving my brother the perfect Christmas gift and how I assumed he'd be disappointed because it wasn't cool enough for his college dorm room and he'd get all moody and mean and our holiday would be ruined.

Catastrophic thinking.

So I cross-examined my thoughts and realized that wasn't the most likely outcome. She had me close my eyes and imagine the best thing that could happen. I imagined Jason loving his gift and then asking me to play a game of chess. (And yes, I imagined that I was wearing a super snazzy business suit for all this. My imagination is very classy.)

Guess what happened! Jason loved his Snoopy calendar and we played chess, but not just one game . . . four games! And we also went to the mall together without Mom, just the two of us having fun and eating waffle fries.

I was wrong to assume my winter break was going to be a disaster. It went amazingly well!

Ms. Benson was right when she said that life can be surprising sometimes—that things can actually turn out better than we ever imagined.

So!

That brings us to January.

It marks the beginning of the year, and I'm excited to get back to Chess Club and the animal shelter. January also means it's my favorite time of year . . . no, not the annual clearance sale at the Yarn Hut—that's *your* favorite time of the year.

For me, of course, it's time for Battle of the Books. My annual tradition! I get to talk to other readers about books. Study the story and characters. Answer reading comprehension questions at a competition. Can you spell H-E-A-V-E-N??

Sign-ups were in October, but I haven't heard much about it since. This explains why I'm so excited because tomorrow—tomorrow!—is the first meeting. It's during lunch, which makes it even more exciting . . . books and food. Who *wouldn't* want to go? I'm sure our librarian, Miss Nikki, has lots of plans to make this amazing. Oh, sheesh, I need to stop calling her Miss Nikki because that's what the kids called her when she worked in the elementary school. I know this because she sometimes volunteers at the public library and I see all the little kids crowd around her. "Miss Nikki! Miss Nikki!" They don't even have actual questions; the kids just like calling out her name. Like she's a rock star.

Now that she's here—in serious middle-school territory—we have to call her by her "proper" name: Miss del Rosario. Which I honestly love so much more. It rolls right off your tongue and into a bowl of luscious chocolate. Sophistication is what I'm going for here.

I'm not sure what will happen at this first meeting. I heard that our middle school has placed last in the competition for three years in a row. I hope we can turn that around since Miss del Rosario is here now. Being on a losing team is . . . well . . . my worst nightmare. But it'll be okay—I have lots of ideas about how we can get everyone to learn the information quickly. Maybe I'll email my ideas to Miss del Rosario.

Oh! Speaking of emails . . . (Note: this next paragraph has nothing to do with emails. It's all about Jackson Whittaker. But you knew that.)

I have some Jackson news. But I'm not even going to tell you about it yet. Getting panicky about conversations with boys is *so* last December. I'll tell you all about it in my next letter.

Cool as a cucumber—that's me.

So tell me everything that's been happening. Every detail! Let's start January off with a notebook celebration! Which means we should meet sometime soon out at the tide pools—our sacred spot. We'll do our best this time to not stand directly under any pelicans flying by.

Let's rock the rest of this sixth-grade year.

Januarily yours,

Olivia

As always, my five gratefuls:

1. This notebook
2. The brand-new sweater I'm wearing tomorrow (Embroidered daisies—total cuteness without, hopefully, any embarrassing sweat!)
3. Battle of the Books
4. Tide pools
5. This notebook (It's a repeat of #1, but it deserves this much admiration.)

Oh! And I've attached our family's Holiday Newsletter. Mom and Dad were so busy that they didn't get around to writing it so I offered to do it. Which is why it was sent out late this year. Also, I'm not sure if I'm doing "Holiday Newsletter!" correctly. Other people seem so cheerful. I just really like numbers and math.

THE WESTON FAMILY'S
ANNUAL HOLIDAY NEWSLETTER

Greetings,

We hope you are having fun. And eating food. And asking your kids a bunch of questions. That's what the holidays are for, right?

Here is our year by the numbers:

31: number of weeks until the Georgia Bulldog football season starts

3: number of chess matches Olivia attended

1574: year of Dad's favorite civilization

6: number of parties Mom held for the University of Georgia football games

14: number of University of Georgia Rice Krispie Treats Olivia consumed

2: number of times Jason visited us from college

1: number of cats named Blinkie that still live with us

We wish you the best this coming year. Hopefully nothing bad happens to you.

The Westons

Hi, friends!

Merry Christmas! I love Christmas card season, because I finally get to put all my skills from the stationery store to good use. Also, I'm hardly ever on the social medias (or computer. I know! I'm awful with technology), so I miss out on updates from everyone. That's what I love about letters—they're a great way to reconnect. In fact, one of my New Year's resolutions is to write more letters. I probably won't, but a mom can dream. :)

We miss you all and hope you had a wonderful year. Here's an update on our little piece of the universe.

The Jorgensen Clan

RUBEN: Ruben is working hard as Mr. Brake. We are opening another shop in Thousand Oaks next year, so he's spent lots of time scouting and hiring. He's also the new Sunday school teacher at our church! Ruben went on an Alaskan fishing trip with college buddies in September . . . just for the halibut (his joke, not mine). He's also started to grow out a beard and I must say, even after twenty years of marriage, he is one handsome guy.

BROOKE: I'm still working part-time at Doodlebug stationery store. I love the store displays and interacting with customers . . . stocking isn't my favorite task. I'm also taking photography classes at Cal Poly, focusing on portraits. And of course, I'm escorting kids to their various activities and sometimes I even get a meal on the table. I love what I do.

LUKE (17): Luke took all-state for the second year in a row in volleyball. He's already looking into schools, and he's only a junior.

Shop Doodlebug!

We spent three weeks last summer checking out different colleges—
he has a favorite but I'm not allowed to say. He's also big into CrossFit.
Still a very accomplished cellist. Grown three inches in one year!

TALIN (14): Oh boy, Talin has blossomed this last year. Such a
beauty. She's also on the straight-A honor roll and growing as a
pianist. She volunteers at the library and the food bank, where she
feeds the homeless during the holidays. She's turning into such an
accomplished, graceful girl.

PIPER (12): Piper is just . . . Piper! She loves playing with her
brothers and helps me with babysitting. I won't even tell you the
name of her favorite TV show, because I'm not totally sure she
should be watching it. :)

FLYNN (3): Funniest kid. Star of his soccer team. Scores goals until
they have to drag him off the field. Still carries blankie everywhere
with him. Random women stop me in the store all the time so they
can touch his curls. Starts art academy with Spencer this spring.

SPENCER (3): Spencer still loves eating vegetables. I could give
him a piece of cake and he would ask for a bell pepper. He knows
178 words in Spanish. It started off with flash cards, but now he
watches language videos and starts a Spanish class next summer. He
is *muy inteligente*!

And that's us! Another year of fun and crazy. Wouldn't change this
group of all-stars for anything.

Merry Christmas to you and yours!
THE JORGENSENS

Dearest, darlingest Olivia,

Why didn't I have you write *our* Christmas card too? I added it to the notebook. I didn't include the family photo because it's just so awful.

This is what you don't see in the family photo: Flynn throwing up three minutes after the picture was taken. Or Talin getting mad at Mom because of the matching plaid shirts. Or the photographer singing the jingle from Dad's Mr. Brake commercial.

What you also don't see is *me*. I'm blocked by Talin's head. Is this supposed to be a metaphor, Olivia? We learned about literary devices in reading. And I'm pretty sure that is a metaphor for my place in the family. Perhaps even my lonely place in the world. This is just like our family fridge.

There's an article from the newspaper when Luke got allstate. There's also a program from Talin's last performance. There are notes from teachers, pictures the twins drew, clips . . . but nothing like that for me. Yes, there are a few photos, but nothing broadcasting my extreme awesome.

That one line keeps echoing in my head. "Piper is just . . . Piper!"

It's like my mom couldn't think of anything else to say about me. All my siblings have these long lists of achievements and Mom makes it sound like I'm some lonely cat lady who watches soap operas all day. (Which, I should mention, is not a bad thing. The plotlines and characters in *Love and Deception* are preparing me for real-life situations. If someone ever goes into a sudden coma or takes on a fake identity, they'll all come running to me for answers.)

I have other things going on. She didn't mention the animal shelter, or LARPing, or knitting. I mean, I had this big birthday party with all these new friends just a few weeks ago. I totally proved that I'm able to make friends, even if my motivation was sort of tied into the Drama! Intrigue! and Scandal! of it all.

And what about my videos?! Guess who documents all of Talin's piano recitals and Luke's games? It's good old Piper-just-Piper with the camcorder I got two Christmases ago. Then I edit those videos so that they're not the most boring things on earth to watch. And when I'm babysitting, so the rest of my family can go out and do all these amazing things, I write and direct videos of my twin brothers. Which, yes, only have twelve views on YouTube, but I've been so focused on the creative side, I haven't done much marketing.

Whew. Okay. I'm not bothered by this. Well, not really. I'm just confused. Nothing I do is very refrigerator-brag-worthy. I don't know how to be more than "just" me. But I'll figure it out. And keep you posted.

Otherwise, Christmas was all:

CARAMEL ROLLS!
SNICKERDOODLES!
HOMEMADE
FUDGE!
STICKY FINGERS!

Oh, and I guess there was family time and presents and yuletide spirits in there, but I thought I would mention the important thing (FOOD) first. The scarves I knit everyone were a hit. You were right to choose the color of yarn that I thought fit their personality. Luke has worn his burgundy one every day of break, and I don't think it's to be nice. It's not like we live in the arctic, so I appreciate the gesture.

Our church class did this Favorite Things party where you bring five of the same item and leave with a basket of random goodies. Of course, my mom—the gift basket queen—was very jealous. I knit beanies, and Bethany almost got in a fight with Tessa over the green one. Which was so sweet! I've never made an accessory so desirable that people almost shed blood trying to get it.

Sorry I couldn't hang out this weekend. Friday I had to do back-to-school chores and babysit the twins. We made a video where I cooked all these weird food combos then recorded the twins eating them and grossing out. Spencer kept saying Spanish words like *"ay, caramba!"*

But it came out as "I kawumby!" Crazy cute.

So far, only nine views, but I could make those kids *stars.*

And finally . . . I'm glad you are excited about school starting again. Of course, that means progress reports come out in the next couple of weeks. I haven't been, um, totally focused on my grades. So I'm a teeny tiny bit worried. What color do you wear when you're worried again? Should I knit a worried-color beanie?

Love you, bestie,

Pipes